Noah Was Haunted By Her Memory.

Thoughts of her interrupted his sleep.

He eyed the door of Martina Logan's condo with a feeling of satisfaction and cynicism. The woman had made love to him like a firestorm for three of the most insane, yet oddly fulfilling weeks of his life, then abruptly disappeared. It became his mission to find her and exorcise her from his mind.

His relief would come from seeing that she wasn't nearly the woman he'd thought her to be. He pressed the doorbell twice.

"Just a minute," her voice called, and his gut twisted at the sound. The door opened, and her eyes met Noah's, her mouth forming an O of surprise.

Noah drank in the sight of her, her dark, tousled hair, shocked blue eyes, long throat, full breasts—and fuller tummy.

Much fuller tummy. Martina was pregnant.

Whose baby? Could it be his? His mind asked the questions, but his gut knew the important answer.

It *was* his baby....

Dear Reader,

Twenty years ago in May, the first Silhouette romance was published, and in 2000 we're celebrating our 20th anniversary all year long! Celebrate with us—and start with six powerful, passionate, provocative love stories from Silhouette Desire.

Elizabeth Bevarly offers a MAN OF THE MONTH so tempting that we decided to call it *Dr. Irresistible!* Enjoy this sexy tale about a single-mom nurse who enlists a handsome doctor to pose as her husband at her tenth high school reunion. The wonderful miniseries LONE STAR FAMILIES: THE LOGANS, by bestselling author Leanne Banks, continues with *Expecting His Child,* a sensual romance about a woman carrying the child of her family's nemesis after a stolen night of passion.

Ever-talented Cindy Gerard returns to Desire with *In His Loving Arms,* in which a pregnant widow is reunited with the man who's haunted her dreams for seven years. Sheikhs abound in Alexandra Sellers' *Sheikh's Honor,* a new addition to her dramatic miniseries SONS OF THE DESERT. The Desire theme promotion, THE BABY BANK, about women who find love unexpectedly when seeking sperm donors, continues with Metsy Hingle's *The Baby Bonus.* And new-comer Kathie DeNosky makes her Desire debut with *Did You Say Married?!,* in which the heroine wakes up in Vegas next to a sexy cowboy who turns out to be her newly wed husband.

What a lineup! So this May, for Mother's Day, why not treat your mom—and yourself—to all six of these highly sensual and emotional love stories from Silhouette Desire!

Enjoy!

Joan Marlow Golan

Joan Marlow Golan
Senior Editor, Silhouette Desire

Please address questions and book requests to:
Silhouette Reader Service
U.S.: 3010 Walden Ave., P.O. Box 1325, Buffalo, NY 14269
Canadian: P.O. Box 609, Fort Erie, Ont. L2A 5X3

Expecting His Child
LEANNE BANKS

Published by Silhouette Books
America's Publisher of Contemporary Romance

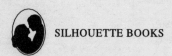 SILHOUETTE BOOKS

ISBN 0-373-76292-5

EXPECTING HIS CHILD

Copyright © 2000 by Leanne Banks

Visit Silhouette at www.eHarlequin.com

Printed in U.S.A.

LEANNE BANKS

is a national number-one bestselling author of romance. She lives in her native Virginia with her husband and son and daughter. Recognized for both her sensual and humorous writing with two Career Achievement Awards from *Romantic Times Magazine,* Leanne likes creating a story with a few grins, a generous kick of sensuality and characters that hang around after the book is finished. Leanne believes romance readers are the best readers in the world because they understand that love is the greatest miracle of all. You can write to her at P.O. Box 1442, Midlothian, VA 23113. An SASE for a reply would be greatly appreciated.

IT'S OUR 20th ANNIVERSARY!
We'll be celebrating all year,
Continuing with these fabulous titles,
On sale in May 2000.

Romance

#1444 Mercenary's Woman
Diana Palmer

#1445 Too Hard To Handle
Rita Rainville

#1446 A Royal Mission
Elizabeth August

#1447 Tall, Strong & Cool Under Fire
Marie Ferrarella

#1448 Hannah Gets a Husband
Julianna Morris

#1449 Her Sister's Child
Lilian Darcy

Desire

#1291 Dr. Irresistible
Elizabeth Bevarly

#1292 Expecting His Child
Leanne Banks

#1293 In His Loving Arms
Cindy Gerard

#1294 Sheikh's Honor
Alexandra Sellers

#1295 The Baby Bonus
Metsy Hingle

#1296 Did You Say Married?!
Kathie DeNosky

Intimate Moments

#1003 Rogue's Reform
Marilyn Pappano

#1004 The Cowboy's Hidden Agenda
Kathleen Creighton

#1005 In a Heartbeat
Carla Cassidy

#1006 Anything for Her Marriage
Karen Templeton

#1007 Every Little Thing
Linda Winstead Jones

#1008 Remember the Night
Linda Castillo

Special Edition

#1321 The Kincaid Bride
Jackie Merritt

#1322 The Millionaire She Married
Christine Rimmer

#1323 Warrior's Embrace
Peggy Webb

#1324 The Sheik's Arranged Marriage
Susan Mallery

#1325 Sullivan's Child
Gail Link

#1326 Wild Mustang
Jane Toombs

Prologue

He thundered across the dusty Texas soil on the back of a black stallion like an avenging angel. Panic flooded her bloodstream. Martina Logan quickly backed away from the crowd of wedding guests and hid behind a tree. The guests at her brother's outdoor wedding gasped and murmured. Not many would be able to identify him from this distance, but Martina could. Her eyes didn't need to tell her; her heart did the trick, pounding erratically against her rib cage.

Noah Coltrane.

Noah slowed the stallion and guided the impressive animal to the vacated dance area. He scanned the crowd and Martina tried to make herself shrink.

Her brother Tyler spoke up. "What do you want, Noah?"

"I'm here to see Martina."

Her stomach dipped to her knees and she prayed he wouldn't see her. She wasn't ready to face him. Not yet.

"She doesn't want to see you," Tyler said. "Get off the property. Can't you see we're having a wedding?"

"That means she's here," Noah said, surveying the crowd once again.

"Buy a vowel," Tyler said. "She doesn't want to see you."

Martina closed her eyes during the long pause that followed.

"I will see her," Noah finally said, the hard resolve in his voice giving her a chill. "Give her that message."

Trembling, Martina stole a private moment and covered her face with her hands. A dozen images raced through her mind. Months ago, hearing Noah's Texas drawl on the stalled El in Chicago had reminded her how far from home she was. Hearing his voice had rubbed at an empty spot, and she had turned around to see the most fascinating man she'd ever met.

Noah was not the usual cowboy. Not only did he rope and ride, he also fenced and traded cattle options on the Chicago exchange. When they'd met, Martina had been temporarily assigned to a computer company in the Windy City while Noah was taking a course in commodities. He'd charmed her and made her feel comfortable before revealing his name.

Martina still remembered the regret she'd felt and seen echoed on his face when they'd realized their families hated each other. There was enough bad blood between the two ranching families to fill the Red Sea. It was bad enough that his family and hers had quarreled for generations over the stream their ranches shared. What sealed the grudge was the fact that Noah's great-grandfather had tried to steal the wife of Martina's great-grandfather, and during the course of it all, the Logan bride had died.

Still, Noah had suggested with a wry chuckle that since they weren't in Texas, they could pretend their last names were different.

He was the biggest no-no she'd ever said yes to. It had been all too easy to fall for him, and the memory of the passion and laughter they'd shared still made her weak. But reality and family loyalty had eventually crept in. Their affair had ended as quickly as it began. Martina, however, had been left with the consequences of her temporary insanity called Noah Coltrane.

Martina bit her lip and opened her eyes. She touched her abdomen swollen with Noah's child. She dreaded the day she would have to face him. She knew it was coming. Noah Coltrane would always be her biggest no-no. Her favorite mistake.

One

He'd finally found her. Six weeks after he'd crashed her brother's wedding, Noah eyed Martina Logan's condo with a feeling of satisfaction and cynicism. The woman had made love to him like a firestorm for three of the most insane, yet oddly fulfilling weeks of his life, then abruptly disappeared.

Her leaving had stung his ego and he hadn't gone after her. He would forget her, he'd told himself. After all, with so much bad blood between their families, they'd both known the relationship was doomed from the start. But he'd seen a fire of independence in Martina's eyes that echoed in his gut, and he hadn't wanted to resist.

As the days passed after she'd left, Noah was haunted by her memory. Thoughts of her interrupted his sleep. It stuck in his craw when he made a few small attempts to locate her and couldn't.

Then it became his mission to find her and to exorcise her from his mind. His peace would come from looking into her eyes and letting her see that she couldn't hide from him. His relief would come from seeing that she wasn't nearly the woman he'd thought her to be. Then he would be on his way.

Walking toward her front door, he idly noticed the scrape of his boots against the hot pavement and the deceptively peaceful sound of birds chirping in the late-spring morning. He paused on her doorstep and, pushing aside the feeling that all hell was about to break loose, he pressed the doorbell twice.

"Just a minute," her voice called, and his gut twisted at the sound. He heard her footsteps and voice grow louder as she came closer.

"Yes, I'm keeping my appointments. I'm fine," she said, opening the door. "I'm—" Her eyes met Noah's and her mouth formed an *O* of surprise. Her jaw worked, but no sound came out. He watched her swallow. "I...I...I've got to go," she said, and pushed a button to disconnect.

Noah drank in the sight of her—her dark, tousled hair, shocked blue eyes, worried mouth, long throat, full breasts and fuller tummy.

Much fuller tummy.

The implication of her change in size triggered a dozen questions inside him. Martina was pregnant.

Whose baby?

Could it be his?

How far along was she?

His mind asked the questions, but his gut knew the important answer.

"I've gained weight," she said, smiling brightly enough to almost blind him. Almost, but Noah noticed the protective way she covered her abdomen with her hand. "You know how that goes. Some people just seem to gain it all in one place." She pushed her other hand through her hair and blinked innocently. "I can't imagine what would bring you here."

Noah struggled with the images that raced through his mind. Images where she had been laid bare beneath him, crying out his name. Images where she had looked into his eyes and he had gotten lost in the depths of her. At the time, he could have sworn she'd been equally lost in him.

"When did you start gaining the weight, Martina?" he asked. "About eight to twelve weeks after the last time you were with me? You must be over six months pregnant."

Her smile slipped slightly. "I don't remember when I started gaining weight," she said.

Another way of pleading the Fifth, Noah thought cynically. "And I'll bet you'll lose a lot of this weight suddenly,'' he said, his emotions roiling like the Galveston beach before a storm.

"The baby's mine, isn't it,'' he said, cutting through her ridiculous story. He decided this situation was going to require the best combination of his instincts and brain.

She dropped her hand from her hair and clasped both of her palms in front of her abdomen. Her gaze narrowed and her eyes glinted with a mixture of fear and fight. "My baby,'' she corrected. "Who told you?''

"No one. I looked at you and knew,'' he said, his entire body clenching with the knowledge that Martina was carrying his baby. "You need to let me in,'' he said, surprised at the calm tone of his voice. He felt as if she had set off a bomb inside him.

Martina bristled. "This isn't a good time. I'm busy working right now. My company is allowing me to design web pages from home, but I do have deadlines.''

"When is a good time?'' Noah asked, baiting her. "Next year?''

Martina's smile vanished and she set her chin. "Next year is too soon.''

It occurred to Noah that this woman could have easily inspired the saying Don't mess with Texas. She tried to close the screen door in his face, but he caught it with his boot. "I'm not going away.''

Her eyes flashed. "I'm over my quota of pushy,

overbearing men in my life. I don't respond well to force.''

He nodded. ''Good,'' he said. ''I only use force as a last resort when I'm dealing with someone who is being unreasonable.''

She looked at him with skepticism, but stepped away from the door.

Martina had dreaded this day. She'd known she would have to tell Noah about the baby someday. She'd decided an e-mail, fax or message sent by carrier pigeon would be much preferable to a face-to-face confrontation. The time had never seemed right. As a rule she didn't procrastinate, but she'd broken several rules by getting involved with Noah in the first place.

As he walked past her, she remembered some of the silly reasons she'd allowed herself to get involved with him. His height. She'd always been tall, and it had felt good to be held by a man several inches taller. She'd liked the way he smelled—of leather and spicy musk. She'd liked the sound of his voice and the way his mind worked.

After living with a father and two brothers determined to protect, defend and dominate her, being with a reasonable man who treated her as an equal had gone to her head like too much tequila.

Martina had the unnerving intuition that she might not be able to count on Noah to be reasonable right now.

He glanced around her den, then walked toward

her. Her heart squeezed in her chest at the formidable expression on his face.

"When were you going to tell me?" he asked in a calm voice at odds with the turbulence in his eyes.

Her stomach fluttered with nerves. "I was going to tell you. I just hadn't figured out how."

"When? After the baby was born? After our child took first steps or went to school? Or reached legal age?"

The sense of betrayal in his voice scraped at her. She struggled with shame and frustration. "I should have told you. It would have been the right thing to do, but it was wrong to get involved with you in the first place. When I found out I was pregnant, I couldn't believe it was true. I had to come to terms with it on my own."

"If you'd told me, you wouldn't have had to do anything alone," he told her.

Martina's heart hurt as a dozen memories slammed through her. "We knew when we got involved that it couldn't last. You said we could pretend while we were in Chicago. You never talked about a future with me because you knew there wouldn't be one."

He rested his hands on his hips. "The baby changes things."

Her stomach sank at the determination in his voice. "For me and maybe for you, but not for us."

"You should have told me."

"Yes, well, I had to get used to the idea first. And

having my brothers find out a Coltrane was the father…'' She broke off and grimaced at the memory of that confrontation.

"What'd they do?'' Noah asked. "Look at you like you were giving birth to the anti-Christ?''

"At first,'' she said. "But I set them straight.''

"Who did you tell them was the father?''

"I told them the stork did it,'' she said, but the flip remark didn't work its charm. "When you showed up at my brother's wedding like the Lone Ranger, it became difficult to deny paternity.'' She took a careful breath. "I have handled this on my own. I got through the shock and morning sickness and everything else on my own. I'm strong. I can handle the rest alone, too.''

He gave a wry half smile that somehow looked dangerous. "We never got around to discussing children, but I have some definite opinions on the subject. The first is that the parents should be married. You and I should marry as soon as possible.''

Martina gaped at him. If he hadn't been dead serious, she would have laughed. "You must not have heard me. I have put up with three domineering men in my life—my father and brothers—and I am not interested in tying myself till death do us part to another.''

"This baby deserves two parents. Both of us will want to be involved in raising the child. I don't walk away from my responsibilities.''

There wasn't an ounce of give in his voice, but

he struck on one issue she'd been unable to resolve in her heart and mind. Martina wanted the best for her child, but she couldn't marry Noah. "We can work out visitation," she began, trying to pump conviction into her tone.

"That's another thing that's stupid. It's crazy for you to live alone here in Dallas when you can live at my family ranch."

Everything inside her balked. "Now I know you're insane. Have you forgotten that my family home borders your property? Do you think my brothers and your brothers are going to have a party over this? I don't think so. Plus, there is the Logan curse. Women bearing the Logan name have shown an annoying tendency to kick the bucket when they fall in love and get married. I'll admit I never thought the curse applied to me, but on the off chance that it does, I have a pretty powerful reason to stay alive and healthy. My baby."

Noah stood there silently. He looked as if he was reining himself in, processing every word she'd said. Planning.

Martina felt a sinking sensation, but kept her back ramrod straight. She was no sissy, she told herself. She could handle Noah Coltrane.

"We'll talk again," he said, pulling out a pen and business card and scratching some numbers on the back of it. "If you need anything, anything at all, call me. Cell number's on the back." He met her gaze again. "You said your family curse means a

Logan woman will die when she marries. You forget. When you marry me, you won't be a Logan woman. You'll be a Coltrane.''

''When cows do algebra,'' she fumed as she watched Noah walk out her door. ''I'll be a Coltrane when Texans stop arguing over water rights, when your brothers and my brothers give each other big hugs, which will be *never*,'' she continued, even though she was only talking to the air that Noah had breathed and the space he had invaded. His presence was still disturbing even though he was gone. ''I'll be a Coltrane when the stars fall over West Texas.''

Noah had so much adrenaline pumping through his veins that he could easily have snapped the steering wheel of his Tahoe in half. He had impregnated the most unreasonable, stubborn woman in Texas, and he had a feeling it was going to take everything he had to corral her and bring her and the baby to the Coltrane ranch where they belonged.

A part of him wondered if the Indian mystic in him had sensed something important had happened to Martina. He wondered if that was what had kept him awake nights. Although Noah knew he was the most modern of the Coltranes, he also suspected the trace of Indian blood in his veins gave him instincts not so easily explained.

He sighed in disgust. It would be nice if those Indian instincts could provide something more useful than a sleepless night, something like an easy way to win Martina over.

To persuade her, he was going to have to see this from her point of view. Noah knew he was more open-minded than his brothers, but he wasn't sure he could think like a woman, God help him. Especially when every drop of primitive protectiveness and possessiveness raged to the surface when he remembered that Martina was carrying his child.

Taking a deep breath, he pulled into the dusty drive to the main ranch house. On a normal day, he felt a sense of well-being every time he came home. Zachary Tremont, former ranch foreman, had always told Noah that if he grew still and quiet, he would hear the voice of welcome when he was in the right place. Zachary was probably the reason none of the Coltrane boys had ended up in prison. Their father, Joe, had been a drunk, a mean one at that, and their mother, a strict churchgoer, had died of cancer. The union hadn't exactly produced a pleasant home environment.

One good thing Joe had done just before he passed away, though, was to hire Zachary. During his time at the Coltrane ranch, Zachary had taught Noah and his brothers the discipline of fencing. More importantly, he had taught each of the boys about honor and the importance of finding and honoring his individual purpose.

Noah missed Zachary and would have traded his most valuable antique sword for a chance to talk to the man now. But Zachary had left when Noah's brother Adam grew old enough to manage the ranch, insisting it was time for him to move on.

Noah glanced at the recently remodeled and expanded ranch house and waited for the feeling of welcome. On a normal day, he felt the warmth of it curl in his stomach and flow through his blood.

This, however, was not a normal day. His brothers were not going to have a party over his news. A riot was more likely.

He waited until everyone had eaten dinner. Adam was downing a third beer, Jonathan was leaning back with his eyes closed, and Gideon was lighting a cigar.

"We need to make plans for an addition," Noah said.

Adam glanced at him quizzically. "Another one? We've already built bunkhouses for the fencing camps and roundup weekends you want to run."

"We can wait. I don't want anyone touching the house," Gideon said. "I'm sick of falling over contractors. I want to smoke cigars in peace."

"Then take them outside," Jonathan muttered, his eyes still closed. He wasn't fond of Gideon's trendy habit.

"It's not a building," Noah said. "It's a baby."

Complete silence reigned. Jonathan's eyes popped open. Adam and Gideon stared at Noah.

"Whose baby?" Adam asked in a low voice.

"Mine," Noah said, and called to the cook.

"Patch, you mind bringing in that good bottle of whiskey and three shot glasses?"

Jonathan, the brother to whom Noah felt closest, had the most even temperament and was by far the most intuitive. "You're not drinking?"

"Not yet," Noah said, and poured the whiskey.

"Congratulations," Gideon said with a sly grin and swallowed his shot. "Does this baby come with a woman?"

"Yeah," Noah said. "Martina Logan."

Jonathan dropped his shot glass. Adam and Gideon stared at Noah in disbelief.

"You better be joking," Adam said.

"I'm not. She's carrying my baby. We met in Chicago. She's not like her brothers," Noah said, then remembered her scorching refusal to his proposal this morning. "In some ways, she's worse," he said with a wry laugh. "But I'm going to marry her, bring her here to live, and we're going to raise the baby here."

Adam and Gideon stood. "You've gone way too far this time," Adam said. "The Coltranes have *nothing* to do with the Logans. We don't date 'em. We don't marry 'em. We don't get 'em pregnant. Hell, we don't speak to 'em."

"Too late," Noah said.

Swearing, Gideon grabbed Noah by the shirt collar. "It's not too late. Tell her to get rid—"

Instinct raged through him, and Noah pushed his

brother away. "I don't want to ever hear that from you or any of you again."

Adam shook his head. "You've gone too far," he said. "I'm cutting you out of the ranch. Just leave and don't come back."

Noah glanced at Jonathan and read the distress and disappointment on his face. His gut wrenched at the thought of leaving. "Okay. I guess that means you don't need the money I make for the ranch by trading cattle futures and leasing the hunting rights."

Adam cursed under his breath. "You know that money has bailed us out during a bad year." He shook his head again. "Now how could you make such a huge mistake?"

"I dislike the Logans as much as you do, but I've been dealt a new hand of cards, and I have to do what's right. We've all spent most of our lives living down the bad decisions our father, or his father, or his father made. I'm not gonna keep making bad decisions. This baby's no mistake."

Adam and Gideon glared at him in hostile silence.

Jonathan sighed and broke the angry, tense silence. "I wonder what Zachary would say right now," he mused in a calm voice that was like cool water on flames.

Noah immediately saw the change in his brothers' faces. Adam exhaled and viewed him with grudging acceptance.

Gideon looked away, clearly ashamed. "Sorry I

said that about getting rid..." He broke off. "Sorry," he said. True to form, he was quick to anger, but usually quick to apologize. "I'm going for a walk."

"I'm going to bed," Adam said.

Noah stood in the dining room with only Jonathan. Jonathan reached for the bottle of whisky, poured a shot into his glass and held it out for Noah to take. "I like a lot of your ideas and innovations," he said. "When Adam balked, I could see you were going to do good things. I always envied how you could think outside the box. But I gotta tell you— this isn't outside the box. It's not outside the county or the state. It's outside the universe. So what was it? Temporary insanity?"

Noah swallowed the liquor, feeling the fire all the way down his throat and chest into his stomach. "Maybe," he said, and met Jonathan's gaze. "It felt right."

Jonathan shook his head in disbelief. "How could it possibly?"

"I'm not sure I can explain it. The same way it feels right for you to train horses. Why aren't you hollering or taking a swing at me?"

Jonathan covered a faint grin with his hand. "Based on my limited experience with the Logans, I'm just guessing that Martina Logan is gonna torture you more than I ever could."

Noah gave a wry chuckle. "Maybe."

"How does she feel about getting married?"

"She's getting used to the idea," Noah said, thinking that wasn't anywhere near the truth. It must have shown.

"She flat out turned you down," Jonathan concluded.

Noah nodded. "She did. But I've had a lot of practice turning no into yes."

Two

___

"**T**hanks for helping with the groceries, Rodney," Martina said as she pushed the key into her front door.

"No problem," her neighbor said. "I— Excuse me, who?"

"I'm the father of her baby," a familiar voice said from behind her, heating her to the core with the simple statement.

Martina's stomach dipped. She had thought he wouldn't be back for at least a week or two. Wishful thinking. She turned quickly and met Noah's gaze, noting the fact that he, instead of Rodney, was carrying her grocery bags.

"What a surprise," she finally managed.

Rodney eyed Noah with suspicion.

"Rodney, this is Noah." She took a deep breath. She rebelled at using Noah's words. They were primal, possessive, and emphasized the connection between them, a connection Martina preferred to diminish. "He, uh, contributed genetic material," she said, and forced a smile. "Thanks again for helping."

"Any time," Rodney said with a nod and curious glance at Noah.

"What brings you here?" she asked Noah after Rodney left.

"You." Noah caught the door for her and followed her into the kitchen. "You missed me," he said, his voice holding a mix of sexy humor.

Martina's lips twitched and she put her bag on the counter. "Like I miss morning sickness."

"Did you have much of it?" he asked more seriously.

"About three weeks when I lived on saltines, soda and vitamins."

"And now?"

She turned to face him. "Now I'm just really big."

His gaze fell over her, lingering on her breasts, tummy and legs. "Just in a few places," he said. "Pregnancy looks good on you."

The way he looked at her reminded her of the passion they'd shared and the way he had taken her body. The way he looked at her reminded her of how much she had wanted him. Martina pushed the thought from her mind and turned back around to put away the groceries. "You didn't really say what you wanted."

"Yes, I did," he said. "You."

Her heart jumped and she nearly dropped a carton of eggs. "You wanted to talk to me about something," she quickly corrected for his benefit and hers.

"Have you thought any more about my proposal?"

She mentally put on her armor as she put away the groceries. "I don't recall any proposals."

"For you to marry me," he told her calmly.

"You didn't ever really ask," she said. "You ordered."

"Will you marry me?"

"No," she said as quickly as he'd asked.

He sighed and she reluctantly met his gaze. "Do you think you are doing the best thing for the baby to not have me involved at all?"

She opened her mouth to say yes, but a strong inner integrity defeated her. She closed her mouth.

"Do you think the best thing for this baby is to have two parents married to each other living in the same home?"

Martina had admired his insight before. Now it got under her skin. "In general, yes, but we have a special circumstance. Our families have held a grudge against each other for over a hundred years."

"What's more important? A grudge or the welfare of our child?"

Martina shook her head. "There's more involved and you know it. You and I wanted each other temporarily. We knew we weren't looking for anything permanent. There's a big difference between what is good on a temporary basis and what is good forever."

Noah walked toward her, his eyes glinting. "Are you saying I'm not good husband material?"

Each step he took closer packed a wallop on her nerve endings. His intensity, his confidence, his personality, his aura had been and still were entirely too sexy for her own good. She lifted her chin. "Yes, I am. There's a big difference between a lover and a husband. As a husband, I can already tell you'll pull the same kind of caveman routines my brothers do. You'll order me around and tell me what to do and expect me to be a good, submissive wife. I'm too independent for that. While you may have been an—" she took a breath and wished for a fan "—incredible lover, you wouldn't work for me as a husband," she said, "at all."

She needed to make that clear to him, to her, to the entire free world, all Third World countries and any planets inhabited by intelligent life.

He put his hands on the counter on either side of her, crowding her. "You're assuming I'll act that

way. You don't know that I will. You really only
have your experience to judge me. So tell me, what
did I do wrong?''

Martina stared into his eyes and bit her lip to keep
from repeating the words that flooded her brain. *You
were too sexy. You made me melt. You made me feel
more like a woman than I've ever felt in my life. You
made me feel like the most desirable woman in the
world. You made me fall so hard I almost couldn't
get back up. You made me feel so much for you so
fast. You terrified me.*

She tore her gaze from his and stared down at his
boots. ''You have the wrong last name. And you
have given signs that you would try to rule me,''
she told him. ''You tried to *order* me to marry you
and come live with you.''

''What was your reaction when you found out
you were pregnant?''

Martina remembered the bloodcurdling scream
she'd let out once she'd left the doctor's office and
closed herself in her car. ''Okay, I'll admit it wasn't
a quiet, rational response.''

''How many decibels?''

She frowned at him. ''I don't know. I just remember wondering if I'd permanently broken my lar-
ynx.'' She smiled. ''But as you can see, I didn't.''

''The point is, your first response wasn't the most
rational. My first instinct was and is to protect.'' His
gaze drifted over her body, warming her. ''What's
wrong with that?''

"Nothing, as long as you don't go overboard."

"And you don't think you'll go overboard protecting our baby?"

Martina's chest tightened. She was already feeling overprotective of the precious life inside her. "It's my job to protect."

"Mine, too," he said, lifting his hand to cup her chin. "I won't forget it," he told her, and everything about him, his voice, his determined eyes, his posture, made an oath.

Martina felt a sinking sensation. This was why she hadn't wanted to tell him. She had known Noah wouldn't abandon his child, and her life would be intertwined with his for the rest of her days. She just wasn't sure she could see him on a regular basis and keep her good sense intact. Lifting her head away, she steeled her mind against him. "That's nice, but—"

"And it's part of the reason I'm here," he said, dropping his hand to his hip, but still crowding her. "There's a lot I don't know about you, and there's a lot you don't know about me. You may not want to marry me, but we're still having a baby together. In that case, we've got a lot to learn about each other."

Martina hadn't thought her stomach could sink any lower. "What are you saying?"

"We need to get to know each other. We need to spend some time together."

No, no, no, no, no. Sliding past him would have

been much easier if she hadn't been seven months pregnant. Martina gently nudged him away. "I hate for you to have to drive so far for something that shouldn't take much time. Don't you think a résumé would work just as well?"

"No."

"We could write each other. E-mail," she said enthusiastically. "Everyone keeps in touch through e-mail these days."

He shook his head. "If this were the Old West, I could haul you off and carry you home. Sadly, in this case, those days are gone," he muttered under his breath. "I know you as a lover. I know what makes you—" his eyes darkened in remembrance "—go," he finished. "But I need to know more than that. I need to know the mother of my child."

His gaze cut through her, and Martina had a terrible premonition that having Noah know her could be more dangerous for her than making love with him had been. His intensity made the prospect feel unbearably intimate. *Oh, hell,* Martina thought, wanting to kick something. How was she supposed to refuse that request?

He moved closer, leaning on his uplifted arm against the wall beside her. "We might as well start with the hard stuff."

Hard stuff, Martina thought. That would be you. "What's that?" she asked warily.

"What's your favorite flavor of ice cream?" he asked.

A rush of relief raced through her. Martina was so relieved she was almost charmed. Almost, but she was determined to stay on guard.

"En garde!" Gideon cried, and lunged toward Noah. Gideon, whose temper flared quickly but cooled with equal speed, had gotten past his anger and was more than willing to try to best his older brother in a duel.

The parry, the clash and scrape of metal swordplay had been one of the best ways for Noah to let off steam since Zachary had taught him and his brothers to fence in the old barn.

"Rough afternoon with the Logan princess?" Gideon goaded him with a smile.

Noah plunged past his younger brother's defense to touch his chest. *He contributed genetic material.* Every time Martina's flip words played through his mind, his head roared with anger.

Gideon nodded wryly at the point and backed away slightly. "I'll take that as a yes."

"It could have been worse," Noah said with a short nod. "Ready?" he asked, and they began again.

"In other words, she didn't sic her brothers on you," Gideon said.

"Compared to Martina, her brothers are cake. We've at least been able to reason with Brock Logan about wandering cattle and the pond we share. Martina knows what's best—she just isn't being reasonable.''

"And what's best is…?"

Noah stated the obvious. "For us to marry and raise the baby here."

Gideon touched his rib cage.

"Touché," Noah said. "Ready."

"Can't blame her for hesitating. We've never been the favored family of the county," Gideon said.

"That's in the past," Noah insisted. It was one of his greatest passions to put the bad Coltrane reputation in the past and to build a new one based on respect. "All of us have worked to put that in the past."

"Yeah, but for Pete's sake, did you have to pick that Logan woman? Why not someone a little more easygoing?"

"You mean a woman who doesn't have the ability to slice a man to ribbons with her tongue?" Noah asked, pushing Gideon closer to the back wall.

"Yeah," Gideon said, swinging his sword for all he was worth.

"Someone more submissive," Noah said, thinking Martina would probably stab them both if she heard this discussion.

"Yeah. It sounds like you might as well be trying to seduce a porcupine," Gideon said. "A pregnant porcupine."

Noah lunged and pressed the tip of his sword to

the protective material covering Gideon's heart. Martina might be acting like a porcupine, but Noah had experienced the soft, giving woman behind the quills. He was determined to find that woman again.

"Touché," his brother said with a shake of his head. "Hell, you make a great case for contraception. What are you going to do?"

"The same thing I do in a fencing match. Find her weakness and exploit it." Noah knew he sounded ruthless, but he wasn't playing for fun with Martina. He was playing for blood, his family name and his child.

He found her reclining on a chaise longue in her backyard in the late afternoon. Dressed in shorts and a maternity tank top she'd lifted above her belly while she rested. Her legs were long and lithe, and knowing the baby she carried was his made him want her in an elemental way. Her expression was soft, almost wistful and her gaze was faraway. He remembered how she had once looked at him with passion-drenched eyes, and he wondered what tender thoughts she could be thinking right now.

He walked closer and heard her say, "I look like a beached whale. I can't even reach my toenails to paint them."

Noah saw the bottle of nail polish beside her, and his gaze shot to the next yard. He saw a woman wearing a bikini. He bit back a chuckle. "You still have the best legs in Texas," he said.

She turned her head quickly, and her cheeks turned pink with embarrassment. "I, uh, was just—"

"—feeling sorry for yourself," he finished for her. "I brought Chinese food for dinner. Does it agree with you?"

Martina sighed. "Unfortunately every food agrees with me now. And I wasn't feeling sorry for myself."

"Uh-huh," he said, without an ounce of conviction.

Martina stood. No, really. I—"

"Martina, you are a very beautiful woman, pregnant or not pregnant. You just haven't had a man around to remind you."

She stared at him for a long moment, revealing a glimpse of the woman he'd known in Chicago. She took a deep breath. "Don't flatter me."

"I won't," he assured her. "I just tell the truth. I'd say something else," he said, allowing his gaze to linger on her full breasts. "But I don't want you to take a swing at me. You might hurt yourself. Are you hungry for Chinese food or not?"

She blinked and paused as if debating whether to hit him, anyway. "I'm hungry, period. Let's eat inside. I didn't expect you," she said, leading him though the back door to the cool kitchen.

"Didn't your mother tell you to always expect the unexpected from a Coltrane?"

Her smile wavered. "My mother didn't get an

opportunity to teach me anything about the Coltranes. She died when I was born.''

Noah immediately regretted his joke. ''I'm sorry. I didn't mean any disrespect.''

''That's okay. Besides, my father and brothers gave me an earful about the Coltranes.'' She plucked the containers of food from the bag.

''I'm sure they did,'' he muttered, and carefully voiced his next thought. ''I realize you descend from Amazons and you could easily harvest an entire field of corn in the morning, deliver your baby at lunch and finish up another field in the afternoon. But do you ever think you might have problems when you deliver the baby?''

She drummed her fingers on the cabinet. ''If you hadn't included the Amazon part, I would say no. But the truth is, although I don't worry about it a lot and the doctor says I'm perfectly healthy,'' she emphasized, ''I think about it every now and then.''

He saw the fleeting vulnerability and longing in her eyes and remembered how he had felt when his mother died. ''You still miss the chance of knowing her, don't you?''

''I would have given anything to know her. I've always missed her and I probably always will. I was lucky to have two brothers who tried very hard and awkwardly at times to make up for the loss.'' She pushed her hair behind her ear. ''What about your parents?''

"I think I miss more of what might have been. My parents weren't happy together."

Martina lifted her eyebrows. "My parents were crazy about each other. My brothers told me that was why my father never seemed happy after she died. Looking at me was too painful for him, because I reminded him of his loss."

Noah realized he had known Martina's mother was dead, but he'd never heard the whole story, and they'd agreed not to speak of their families during their time together in Chicago. It made him see her in a new light. "We had a foreman named Zachary, who taught my brothers and me about being a man. Zachary always said the strongest love survives distance and death, and it always makes you a better man."

She narrowed her eyes. "Are you saying my parents didn't love each other?"

"I'm saying your dad missed an opportunity to love and be loved by a little girl who could have taken away some of the hurt."

Martina looked at Noah for a long moment. He could practically see her mind poking at his statement, examining and pondering, then setting it aside. She glanced at the boxes of food on the counter. "Dibs on the sweet 'n' sour chicken."

They dug into the food, and Martina didn't eat nearly as much as Noah had expected. "I thought you were eating for two. You made it sound like you're eating everything but the living-room furniture."

"I'm not eating for two. It's more like I'm eating for one and one-twelfth. Besides, I wanted to save room for ice cream." She smiled with mischief. "I need my calcium."

"Have you had an ultrasound yet?"

She nodded as she scooped fudge-swirl ice cream into two bowls. "Two months ago. The way the baby was positioned didn't reveal its sex, but I have a feeling it will be a—"

"—girl," he interjected.

"—boy," she said at the same time with a look of surprise on her face.

"I would have thought you'd have some sort of macho expectation about producing a male," she said.

"And I would have thought you'd have some sort of feminist expectation about producing a female," he said. "Both wrong about each other. Looks like we've got a long way to go to get to know each other."

Her face fell. "I still think e-mail is the best solution."

"It hasn't been that bad this time," he said, rising from his chair and walking closer to her. Following an impulse that could get him kicked, bitten or scratched, he lifted her finger to his lips and sucked the ice cream from the tip. Her eyes grew wide and she jerked her hand from his.

"What has made you more reasonable this time?" he asked. "Maybe you like me a little more than you thought you did."

She took a quick breath and a dozen emotions swept through her blue eyes. Noah would swear one of them was desire. Maybe he was getting through.

"Food," she said. "It was definitely the food."

It was definitely not the food that was keeping her awake tonight, Martina thought much later as she threw back the covers on her bed. Every time she closed her eyes, a picture from the first time she and Noah had made love flashed across her mind.

She sat up in bed and sighed, holding her head in her hands and surrendering to the memory for just a moment. They'd eaten Chicago pizza for dinner, then Noah had taken her back to his suite to show her how he traded futures on the Chicago exchange on his laptop. His excitement had been contagious, and after a while, she'd been more caught up in his enthusiasm than his words.

"You're not listening," he said, sitting beside her, his thigh rubbing against hers.

Martina felt her cheeks heat. "I was," she insisted.

"Okay, what happens after the price jumps ten percent?"

"I didn't know there'd be a quiz."

He laughed, and the rich, dark sound curled inside her and heated her down to her toes. He tugged her from her chair and pulled her onto his lap. "If you weren't thinking about futures, then what were you thinking about?"

Bracing herself on his shoulders, she considered dodging the question, but followed another instinct, instead. "I was thinking about you," she said, lifting her fingers to his solid jaw. "You have such a passion for almost everything you do."

His eyes darkened and he pressed her fingers to his lips. "More than one person has called me crazy for my ideas."

"A little crazy is not a bad thing," Martina said, feeling a relentless urgency grow in her belly and blood.

He sucked her finger into his mouth, and she held her breath while he held her gaze. "I'm getting a passion for Martina."

"That could be too crazy," she whispered as he pulled her face closer to his.

"Too late," he said, and took her mouth.

Martina's world spun. He had kissed her before, but tonight was different. She felt it in the air, in his touch, inside her. He made love to her mouth, tasting her, seducing her, savoring her until her heart clamored for more. She sank her fingers into his hair, luxuriating in the soft, wavy texture.

He pulled away and she felt almost as if she was in a dream. Giving her a dozen opportunities to stop him, he slowly, deliberately lifted her sweater over her head and unfastened her bra.

"Do you want this?" he asked, touching the aching tips of her breasts with his thumbs.

Her mouth went dry and she closed her eyes. Her heart hammered a mile a minute. There were reasons, very valid reasons, she should stop, but her brain could not produce one of them at this moment. She had never wanted a man so badly in her life. It wasn't so much his incredible body as much as it was his mind, his very being. The way he thought, the way he acted.

"Yes," she said, the honesty coming from deep inside her. "I want you."

He dipped his mouth to one of her nipples and took it into his mouth.

Fire had raced through her, and Martina had bitten back a moan. He would consume her, she'd thought, and a lick of apprehension had mingled with the heat of her desire. He would learn more about her tonight than any man ever had. She would have to keep a part of herself from him. He must never know, she'd decided, that he was her first.

Distress crowded Martina's throat, and a soft sound escaped, breaking her reverie. Somehow she had been convincing enough that Noah hadn't guessed. He had been so caught up in their passion that he still didn't know he had been her first. Unable to sit still one second longer, she rose from her bed. She needed to leave these memories behind, to exorcise them, if only temporarily, from her mind.

She instinctively walked toward the nursery. She

hadn't bought a crib or even painted the baby's room yet. The only piece of furniture in the room was a toy chest full of odds and ends she'd begun to collect. She knelt beside the light oak chest and touched the infant sleepers, receiving blankets, a stuffed bear, then brought out the little box that made her heart contract and expand every time.

Baby booties.

It was the silliest thing, but the tiny, tiny white booties made it all feel real and right to her. Seeing Noah tonight had confused her, and she didn't need to feel confused. Martina knew what she had to do. She had to keep her head together and love and raise this baby. She had to resist the urge to lean, especially on Noah. He made her think. Every time he visited her, there was more to like, more to admire, more to want and, in turn, more to fear.

The thought of knowing him more made every muscle in her body tense. It wasn't just that he was a Coltrane, although heaven knows that was enough. Martina had a feeling in her heart, in her blood, that if she fell for Noah, his being was so big and powerful that he would swallow her and she would simply disappear.

Three

___

"**H**ave you heard anything from—" Martina's sister-in-law, Jill asked "—your assistant procreator?"

Martina grinned as the two women carried the results of their shopping trip into her condo. "I like that. Takes a lot of the messy emotion out of it?"

"I wouldn't want to upset the mother-to-be."

"By using expressions like former lover, or father of my child, or one of the top five men my brothers most hate." Martina gritted her teeth. "Thank you."

"Hate is a strong word," Jill said, revealing her public-relations background. "Your brothers may not really hate Noah Coltrane. They don't even know one another."

"They hate him," Martina said, stomping upstairs to the nursery. "Brock hates him because he's a Coltrane and one of their bulls jumped the fence and had entirely too much fun with some of our heifers. It made calving season a real pain because the bull was the wrong size and some of the calves were too big, and then there's your husband, Dr. Tyler Logan, who used to get into fistfights with Noah on a weekly basis when they were in their teens. And then there's the small matter that Noah got their baby sister pregnant. Yeah, I would say his name is dirt."

"But people change and they haven't truly sat down and talked since they became adults."

"That's to prevent bloodshed and eventual death by lethal injection. Texas believes in capital punishment."

Jill chuckled and put her arms around Martina in a hug. "Don't you think you're exaggerating just a little?"

"No," Martina muttered. "And I'm not exaggerating when I say how nice you are to check on me and go baby shopping with me." Martina knew Jill was unable to bear children because of an injury from an automobile accident, and her sister-in-law's continued generosity often brought tears to her eyes. Jill hadn't allowed her injury to prevent her from being a mother to a child who needed her. She and Tyler had adopted a son as soon as they got married.

Jill's watery gaze met Martina's damp one and

both women laughed. "At least you can blame this on hormones. I'm really okay. It's amazing what marrying your brother and adopting Sam have done for me. I just want you and your baby to be healthy and happy." She sobered. "And I notice you didn't answer my question about your assistant procreator."

Martina made a face. "Yes. He found me." She pulled bumper pads and sheets with a soothing cloud motif from a bag.

"And?"

"And he immediately said we should get married, and I told him never, and he said we need to get to know each other, and I suggested e-mail."

"You must have felt something for him to get involved with him," Jill said.

Martina didn't like being reminded of her initial attraction to Noah. It had been strong and sexual, and she wasn't feeling very sexy these days.

Her doorbell rang, saving her from responding.

"Pizza," a male voice called.

Martina felt a twinge. The voice was familiar. "I didn't order pizza," she muttered, rising from the floor. Although pizza sounded like a good idea.

Jill joined her at the top of the stairs. "Your pizza-delivery guy looks a lot different from mine."

Noah had let himself in her unlocked door. His intense gaze wrapped around Martina and squeezed before he gave a slight grin that made her stomach flip. How had he known she would be hungry? Martina rolled her eyes at herself. When was she *not* hungry?

"What a surprise," she said in a neutral voice, walking down the stairs.

He flipped open the lid to reveal a large, hot pizza with mushrooms and onions. She eyed him suspiciously. "How did you know they're my favorite toppings?"

"It's my job to know," he said in a voice that would melt brick.

Martina tried to ignore the way her heart sped up.

"You're the man who arrived on horseback at Brock and Felicity's wedding," Jill said, her eyes growing wide in realization. "The fa—" She stopped and appeared to correct herself. "The fellow procreator."

Noah's jaw tightened. "Noah Coltrane. I'm the father of Martina's baby. And you?"

Martina ground her teeth. "This is my sister-in-law, Jill. She's married to Tyler."

"A pleasure," Noah said, shifting the pizza box so he could shake hands.

Jill nodded, still neutral. "You come bearing pizza?"

"I understand pregnant women get hungry," he said in the same sexy voice that made Martina feel hungry in all ways. "Satisfying Martina's appetite is my job."

Jill's lips twitched. "Something tells me you're up to the challenge." She glanced at Martina. "I should run and leave you two to your appetites and pizza.''

"No. You don't have to go. There's plenty for—''

"I really need to get back.'' She gave Martina a quick hug and whispered, "Enjoy yourself. It's not as if you can get pregnant.''

Shocked, Martina gaped at Jill. *Traitor!* "Tyler would not appreciate that comment.''

"He may eventually,'' Jill said. "Take care and call me for anything.''

"Yes, but—'' Martina watched her sister-in-law smile and leave. She turned to Noah and scowled.

"Nice lady,'' he said cheerfully. "How are you?''

"I'm retaining water.''

Looking down at her from beneath his black Stetson, he nodded. "I can take care of a lot of things, but probably not water retention. Pizza?''

"Yes,'' she said, and added dutifully, "thank you.''

"My pleasure.'' He strolled into the kitchen in front of her, giving her an unobstructed view of his impressive backside. A memory flashed in her mind of the time Noah had coaxed her into making love in front of a mirror. The images of her naked body and his and the passion between them were so hot she prayed her thoughts didn't show on her face.

Noah turned and studied her. "Are you okay? You look flushed.''

Darn. "Heating for two.'' Martina smiled and

headed for the freezer. She opened the door and stuck her face inside to cool her cheeks as she pulled out some ice cubes.

She dumped the ice into two glasses and grabbed a couple of soft drinks. "How are you managing to get your work done and take time out to visit me?"

"I keep my trading to a minimum on the day I see you and work on my other projects on the weekends. I can handle it," he assured her in that low, sexy voice.

Martina's gaze skimmed over his broad shoulders. Yes, he could probably handle just about anything he wanted. "You don't really need to visit so often," she said.

"Sure I do. You'd miss me," he mocked.

"Oh, I don't think—"

"Have some pizza," Noah interjected. "I have a surprise for you after you finish eating."

"What kind of surprise?" she asked, immediately curious.

"It's little."

"What is it?"

"Now if I told you, it wouldn't be a surprise."

She gave a much-put-upon sigh.

Noah's smile twitched with humor. "Your impatience reminded me a little of my brother Gideon."

"I don't know much about Gideon. Come to think of it, I don't know much about any of your brothers."

Noah simply nodded and ate a slice of pizza.

"Well?" she prompted. "Are you going to tell me about your brothers?"

"I didn't know you were interested in my family."

I'm not, she opened her mouth to say, but immediately knew it wouldn't have been the truth. She was far more interested in Noah and his world than she should be. "I read an article about how a baby shares genes with the sisters and brothers of the mother and father, so it would probably be a good idea, as a mother, for me to know about your brothers."

"Uh-huh," he said, his expression a mixture of disbelief and amusement.

The amusement bothered her more than the disbelief. "You don't take me seriously, do you?" she asked. "You are tremendously amused by me, aren't you?"

His expression immediately turned deadly serious. "You may have a great sense of humor, Martina, but I have always taken you seriously—as a lover and now as the mother of my child."

Martina felt a shiver at the intensity in his expression. She often had the sense that by getting involved with Noah, she might as well be stepping into a hurricane. She was drawn to Noah's dynamic energy and the calm center he seemed to possess, but she always found herself wondering how she could put one foot in and keep her other foot out.

She still wondered how she could be involved with him and keep herself.

"But you want to know about my brothers," he said. "Adam is the oldest. He is quiet and traditional. He manages the cattle on the ranch. His temper is more of a slow burn. He's very serious and could afford to lighten up every now and then. My brother Jonathan is the peacemaker. He raises and breaks horses. He rarely gets angry at anyone other than himself. Gideon is a pistol. He has a quick temper, but he doesn't hold a grudge. He loves a good challenge."

"It sounds like all of you stick together."

Noah made a wry face. "For the most part, we've had to, what with our dad's problem. But we've been known to use our fists to persuade."

Martina couldn't help noticing Noah's hands, which were clasped together. She knew that when he was a young teen, he'd gotten into many fights. Part of what intrigued her about him was the way he had left his anger behind. She wondered how he'd done that. "Your father's drinking problem?"

"Yep. That and some of the other things our forebears have done. The Coltranes have a reputation to live down and another one we want to build. All of us want that."

"What was it like being the black sheep of the county?"

"Good and bad. Mostly bad. Teachers, neighbors, mostly everyone expected the worst when a Coltrane came around. So we often lived down to the expectations. That just ended up causing more trouble. Then my dad hired a foreman. His name was Zachary and he taught us how to fence and turned us into modern-day knights.''

Martina blinked. ''Modern-day knights? I knew all of you fenced. People were always afraid one of you might stick a sword in someone who ticked you off.''

''There's that Coltrane rep again. Zachary started us out with wiffel bats. It was a big deal when he let us use one of his swords, and the biggest deal was when he gave us each a sword. We had to earn it,'' Noah said with a faraway look in his eyes.

''How did you earn it?''

''Grades, self-control, attitude and skill with the sword.''

It was difficult for Martina to keep her objections against Noah intact when she pictured his transformation from an angry teen to a man. ''I never heard anything about this.''

''Most people haven't. Zachary left the ranch a few years ago. He told us we had the tools. We would always know what to do.''

''You miss him,'' Martina said in surprise.

Noah nodded. ''Yeah, I do.''

''You've described your brothers,'' she ventured, picking up her second slice of pizza. ''How would they describe you?''

''Besides a pain in the ass,'' Noah said with a

wicked grin, "the driven dreamer, the one who is always trying to do impossible stuff."

"Impossible stuff like what?"

"Like trading cattle futures and making money at it. Running weekend roundups and increasing the ranch's revenue. Starting a fencing camp." He paused and met her gaze. "Trying to marry the Logan princess."

Martina felt as if she'd been punched by the look of determination on his face. Her heart hammered against her rib cage. "You want to marry me because I'm carrying your..." She broke off, refusing to use the words that sent her into a spin every time. "Because the baby I'm carrying has some of your genes. You don't want to marry me because you love me. You don't want me to come live with you because you can't live without me."

His eyes flashed with anger. "It would be tough finding that out now. When you left, you didn't give either of us much choice."

Her chest tightened. "I was just a fling for you."

"Martina, you are not fling material." His nostrils flared slightly and he narrowed his eyes. "Was it so easy to leave?"

His words echoed inside her, sending her perspective in circles. She had survived the past seven months by believing that what she and Noah had shared was a fling. She'd chanted it to herself day and night. "One of us had to do it. It had to be done."

"Why?"

Martina fought the jittery feeling spreading throughout her. She stood and tossed her napkin into the trash. "Because of our families. One of us had to stop it before we got in too deep."

She felt Noah behind her. "Did you succeed? Did you stop before we got in too deep?"

His question taunted her heart while his breath teased the back of her neck. She closed her eyes and mentally put her brick wall back in place. She turned and lifted her chin. "I think the general consensus is that I didn't get out unscathed," she said, putting her hand on her abdomen. "You said something about a little treat? Is it a brownie?"

He tilted his head to one side and shook it. "No." He waved his hand toward the chair. "Have a seat."

Curious, she sat and guessed again. "Cookies?"

He shook his head.

"Not cake or pie?"

He laughed. "No more food this time." He knelt beside her, and shock and alarm crowded her throat.

"Oh, no," she said. "You're not going to ask—"

"—for your hand," he finished. "No. I'm asking for your foot."

She frowned. "My foot?"

He slipped her sandal off her foot before she could say, *You are nuts.*

"If you won't trust me with your hand, will you trust me with your foot?"

"As long as it doesn't involve any weapons."

"Just one," he said, pulling a bottle of nail polish from his pocket. "But it won't hurt."

Four

"Are you crazy?"

Noah held fast to Martina's foot as she tried to pull it back. "Not at all. You were crying over the fact that you couldn't reach your toes. What's a former lover good for if he won't paint your toenails every now and then?"

Martina gasped, her eyes wide with shock, her mouth moving, but nothing coming out.

It was a nice change, Noah thought. He liked her off balance. There was something incredibly sexy about the color in her cheeks, the spark in her blue eyes and the tremble of her full mouth. He knew how that mouth tasted.

She shook her head as if to shake herself out of her state of shock. "I wasn't crying," she said.

"Okay, whining," he corrected.

She opened her mouth again, then snapped it shut and glowered at him. "I don't like being called a whiner."

Noah pulled a chair over to sit down and prop her foot between his legs. "Good thing I didn't do that."

"You said whine."

"Big difference. Whiner is a noun that suggests a person who whines frequently. Whine is a verb that could indicate a one-time or infrequent occurrence." He opened the tiny bottle and lifted the brush. "Any tips? I've never done this before."

"First you wipe the excess off the brush inside the bottle. Why are you doing this?"

He painted her big toenail. "I told you. You," he said, dipping the brush again, "expressed unhappiness over not being able to paint your toenails."

"Why didn't you just pay for a pedicure?"

He glanced up at her and smiled. "That wouldn't be nearly as much fun. I bet a man has never done your toenails."

"Yes, a man has."

Noah paused, feeling a surprising slice of jealousy. He glanced up at her. "Who was that?"

"Tyler," she said, and smiled. "He always had a steady surgeon's hand."

A surge of relief trickled through Noah when he

heard her brother's name. He wasn't at all comfortable with the range of emotions Martina generated inside him. As much as she should be his, she wasn't. He continued to paint her toenails in silence.

"Nice color," she said after he started on her other foot.

"I did research," he murmured, thinking that even her feet were sensual—long and delicate.

She jerked slightly. "Research?"

"Don't move," he warned. "You don't want azalea pink all the way up your foot. Yes, I did research, but I won't reveal my sources." Martina's sister-in-law Felicity had asked him as many questions as he'd asked her the day they'd shared coffee.

"But I want to know."

"Fine," he said, not missing a beat as his gaze met hers. "Let me stay the night."

She blinked and he watched her swallow. "I can't imagine why you would want to stay the night with a woman who is seven months pregnant."

"I can think of some reasons," he said, holding her gaze. "Would you like me to tell you them?

"I'd like to see you naked in the moonlight with your belly swollen with my baby. I'd like to touch you with my hands and mouth. I'd like to—"

"No!" Martina shook her head and put her hands to her ears. "No. I don't want you to tell me reasons, and you don't need to tell me your source because you're not staying the night."

"Why not?" he asked, applying a second coat of polish. "Has pregnancy made you chicken?"

"No," she said. "It's made me more sensible."

Noah silently pondered her response as he finished the second coat. Then he skimmed his fingers up the sole of her foot and looked up at her. "You have pretty feet."

Her toes curled and he grinned. "You're welcome."

She looked at him with flashes of wariness and wonder, sensuality and seduction in her startling blue eyes. "It would be easier for both of us if you would just be yourself, instead of being so..." She broke off, her finely arched eyebrows furrowing.

"So what?" He linked his fingers around her slim ankle.

"So kind," she said. "It would be better for you to just be yourself."

His lips twitched. "And that would be?"

"Domineering, pushy, superior, overprotective."

"Is the who I was in Chicago?"

She faltered and looked down. "No, but I'm sure the prospect of fatherhood brings out buried qualities in a man."

He sighed, wondering how he was going to get through to her. He had known her when she was soft and open to him. He remembered that Martina and knew she was still inside. Her softness and openness were just locked away from him.

He stood between her legs and leaned forward,

nudging her chin upward with his finger so he could see her eyes. "I wish I knew what you were afraid of."

Bingo. Her eyes widened and she sucked in a sharp breath. The air between them seemed to thicken and crackle. "I'm not afraid."

Noah didn't believe her and although she might be mad as hell at him, he wasn't backing down. "Keep saying it, Princess Logan." He dipped his head close enough to brush his lips over hers, close enough to remind both of them what they'd once shared. "Maybe you'll believe it." He grabbed his hat from the table. "Sleep well."

Martina sat in her kitchen fuming as she waited for her toenails to dry. Noah Coltrane was an egotistical jerk, pretending that he wanted to seduce her, then insinuating that she was *afraid*. Not just afraid in general, she suspected, but afraid of him. She made a scoffing sound that only her goldfish could have heard if it had had ears.

She glanced down at her azalea-pink toenails and felt herself soften. The man had painted her toenails. If she tried to explain this to anyone else, she would sound like a nut. But the experience had been oddly intimate. Her foot resting between his legs, brushing his strong inner thighs, had reminded her of the passion they had shared. His determination to do a perfect job had reminded her of his determination to push her to the heights of pleasure.

She wasn't afraid. She was terrified.

What if she couldn't resist Noah? What if she fell in love with him? What if she fell so helplessly in love with him that she gave in and married him and spent the rest of her life trying to make him love her? She knew he didn't love her. He liked her and perhaps in some strange way desired her, but her primary value to him was the fact that she carried his child. His motivations for marrying her were all admirable and honorable, but they didn't involve love.

Martina didn't like the idea of being the only one in over her head here. If she was going to be vulnerable and head over heels in love, then she wanted Noah to feel the same way. It seemed fairer that way. Plus, she'd spent too many years trying to gain equal ground with the men in her life; she didn't want to spend the rest of her years doing the same thing.

Martina shuddered, then stood and walked gingerly toward her computer room. She'd had very good reasons for running from Noah seven months ago, and those reasons were still valid. She put her hand on her abdomen and sighed. Unfortunately, she had an even bigger reason she could no longer run from him. She just wondered how she could keep from falling in love with him.

Martina wasn't exactly sure how it happened, but Noah managed to join her for her first childbirth-preparation class. As they pulled into the parking lot of her doctor's building, she turned to him. "If anyone asks, we are not married. I don't want anyone misinterpreting your presence."

He ignored her and got out of the truck. Martina followed his lead and started to get out of her side. Her foot slipped and she started to fall. A thin slice of panic cut through her.

Noah's arms closed around her and he pulled her against him. "Don't do that," he said.

"Don't do what?" she asked, hiding her own jittery nerves. "I had to get out of your truck."

"Just wait for me to help you," he said irritably, his jaw tight with tension. "Don't let your mile-wide independent streak end up hurting you or the baby."

His accusation stung. It felt so good to be held by him at the same time that his words hurt her. "You don't really think I would do anything to hurt the baby."

He loosened his grip and the fierce glint in his eyes faded. "I don't think you'd do anything to hurt the baby. I want you to be careful with yourself. I'm not around as much as I'd like to make sure you're okay."

"I'm okay," she insisted as much for herself as for him. "I'll be okay."

He released her, but stayed close as they walked into the doctor's office. The lobby was used as the classroom and several couples were already seated. A nurse approached Martina with a folder.

"Hi, I'm Emily Ross and I will be your teacher for the next several weeks. You are?"

"Martina Logan and—"

"And you must be Mr. Logan," Emily said with a smile.

"No," Martina and Noah said at the same time.

"His name is Noah Coltrane," Martina said. "We aren't married."

"But I plan to change that," Noah said.

Emily's smile broadened. "Oh. Well, welcome to the class."

Martina frowned at him. "Did you have to tell her that?"

He shrugged, momentarily distracting her. She wished he wouldn't do that. The simple movement conjured up images of nights when she had traced the contours of his shoulder muscles with her hands and mouth. *Stop it,* she told herself.

"Would you rather I tell her you were the best lover I'd ever had and I have every intention of making you mine for good?"

Martina blinked and her stomach filled with butterflies. "If that were true," she said, "then you would have sought me out before seven months had passed."

"I did," he said. "Your employer said you were doing Web design from your home, there was no forwarding address or phone number from your previous apartment, and no one in West Texas seemed to know where you were. And for some reason your brothers weren't inclined to discuss your whereabouts with me."

Martina stared at Noah, feeling an odd knot of emotion form in her throat. Looking into his eyes, she could almost believe that her leaving abruptly had mattered to him. But that couldn't be, she told herself. He'd been so light about their relationship, so firm about not discussing the future. He'd teased her out of her clothes and into his bed so quickly it had made her head spin. Every time she was around him, it seemed he made her head spin.

Gulping over her tight throat, she shook her head. "You told me one of the things you liked most about our relationship was that neither of us had any long-term expectations. You told me that the last night we spent together."

He narrowed his eyes. "Neither of us knew what we had, what we could have."

Her heart ached, but she needed to remind him and herself. "And we'll never know now," she said firmly, and looked around for a seat. "Time for class."

Throughout the session, Martina felt Noah's gaze on her, but she tried to concentrate as the instructor gave a brief overview of the warning signs and stages of labor, and instructions on sex during pregnancy. When Martina looked at her full abdomen, she wondered if she would ever have sex again.

When she thought about the warning signs of complications, she thought about her mother.

She wondered if her mother had felt a premonition about her pregnancy or if she'd been eagerly looking forward to the birth of her third baby. Martina knew her mother's death had been a complete shock to her father and brothers.

A familiar longing swept over her. Lately, not a day passed that Martina didn't wish she could talk to her mother. Noah touched her arm, shaking her out of her reverie.

"You're supposed to be breathing," he whispered.

"I was," she told him.

He shook his head. "Deep breathing for relaxation. First stage of labor."

Martina glanced at the teacher and put aside her distracting thoughts. If she didn't focus on the class, Noah was going to know more about going through labor than she did, and she would *never* live that down.

After class, they drove home in silence. He pulled into her driveway, but didn't get out. "You're quiet."

She smiled. "Rare, isn't it?"

He nodded. "What's on your mind?"

She shrugged. "Lots of things. Labor, delivery, wondering what it was like for my mother."

His gaze turned thoughtful and he squeezed her shoulder. "Worried?"

"Not really," she automatically said. "There's no reason—" She broke off and smiled at the sensation of her baby's movements.

"What is it?"

"I think we've got a rodeo rider." She pressed her hand against her belly and saw the look of curiosity and longing on Noah's face. The expression moved her. Impulsively, she put his hand on her belly.

His eyes widened. "Hell, she's active!"

Martina laughed. *"He,"* she corrected.

"She," he corrected, then cradled her belly with both hands. "Does she do this all the time?"

The fascination in his voice did strange things to her heart. "Not all the time. He sleeps some, but sometimes it feels like he's gearing up for a rodeo."

Noah stroked his fingers over the blouse covering her. The gesture was oddly tender and sensual. "I know this has been happening for centuries, but it still feels like a miracle. You and I made this magic happen."

With dark eyes, he held her gaze for a long moment, a moment where something inside her seemed to creak and shift.

Martina wasn't sure there were words for what his eyes were saying to her. Noah leaned closer and she held her breath. He dipped his head and slowly, softly rubbed his warm lips over hers.

Martina felt the caress electrify her nerve endings from her head to her toes. He kissed her and a hundred emotions tumbled through her. All the passion they'd shared and something more powerful jerked at her like a game of crack the whip.

Alarm shot through her. She pulled back, staring at him, waiting to breathe. Martina lost herself in his changeable eyes. Sometimes green, occasionally blue and in rare moments gray like a storm-tossed sea, his eyes truly seemed to mirror the inner man. He was one man, yet had such diversity, a diversity that had fascinated her from the moment she'd met him. Strong, rugged, intelligent, intuitive.

Perhaps too intuitive, she thought. Sometimes she feared he could see everything going on inside her. "I need to go," she whispered, and turned away from him.

She didn't make it out of the car before he appeared by her side. He cupped her elbow, and though she felt the urge to wrest her arm from him, Martina knew it would have been childish. Still, just his touch set off a riot inside her. She'd run from the intimacy they'd shared, but his closeness stirred up images of his hands exploring and pleasuring her.

"You haven't forgotten, have you?" he asked in a low voice as they reached her porch.

"Forgotten what?" she returned, digging for keys in her purse.

"What it was like when you were mine."

Her heart slammed into overdrive. "I was never yours."

Noah boldly lifted his hands beneath her cotton

blouse and touched the bare flesh of her belly. "Yes, you were. There's plenty of proof. Here," he said, then skimmed his hand up between her breasts. "And here. You were mine."

Five

___

You were mine.

Noah's words echoed through Martina's head as she fell into a fitful sleep. The images seeped inside her, at first hazy around the edges.

He set her on the desk in his hotel room with a playful, yet intent gleam in his eye. Martina's heart fluttered and she wondered what was next. He was always surprising her.

He skimmed his finger up the inside of her stocking-clad leg all the way to her knee. "I've always thought the man who invented panty hose should have been horsewhipped."

She grinned. "And why is that? Do you think it would be better for women to freeze?"

"No," he muttered. *"But there are better ways to keep warm."* He continued to slide his finger up the inside of her thigh. When he encountered bare skin, surprise flickered across his face and he met her gaze. *"The person who invented thigh-highs is due a thousand thank-yous."* He lowered his mouth to hers and said against her lips, *"You keep surprising me."*

Martina swallowed all her doubts and lost herself in his kiss. She was totally out of her depth with this man and could only hope she was concealing that fact. He slid his tongue over hers, teasing her to give him what he wanted. Her entire body clamored in response. Her breath grew short, her nipples tightened, and she grew moist and swollen.

Back and forth Noah rubbed the exposed sensitive skin of her inner thigh. He thrust his tongue into her mouth, mirroring the way he had taken her more intimately at other times. Hot and restless, Martina suckled his tongue deeper.

Noah shuddered and pulled back slightly. *"Everything about you is one big tease for me."* He pushed her skirt farther up her legs and dipped his fingers beneath the edge of her panties. *"You're the apple I'm not supposed to eat, but tasting you isn't enough. I want all of you."*

The mixture of overwhelming frustration and desire in his voice echoed inside her. Although neither she nor Noah ever spoke of their families, the long-standing grudge stood between them, a silent, strong barrier that prevented them from getting as close to each other as they wanted. Martina wanted him. She wanted to drink his words and endlessly explore his mind. She wanted to make him ache the same terrible delicious way he made her ache.

Whenever he kissed her, the air around them seemed to grow thick, just as it did before a storm. She felt that same impending sense that something powerful was going to happen. When they made love, it always did inside her. Martina struggled with the strange feeling that her premonition represented something larger than this moment, but her mind grew cloudy with passion.

Impatient with the obstacles between them and the restraint that kept her from being with him fully, she pushed all thoughts of her family and his aside. She ruthlessly banished everything but him from her mind.

Tugging at the buttons on his shirt, she pulled it open and ran her hands over his warm, solid chest. Instinct driving her, she slid her fingers down to the top of his jeans and pulled his belt loose. She brushed her open mouth against his, then slid her lips down his throat to his chest. She dipped her hands beneath his jeans to where he was hard and aroused.

He sucked in a sharp breath, and his eyes narrowed. ''What do you want?'' he asked, his fingers exploring her soft, damp secrets. ''Do you know what you want, Tina?''

The tension in her core and mind tightened, and she felt hot inside and out. Had she ever wanted this much? Staggering desire and fear mingled. She swallowed, shoving the fear away. "I want you," she said, hearing the telltale huskiness in her own voice. "I want everything."

Her words seemed to make him combust. He pulled her panties away so that she was bare beneath him. Gazing at her naked femininity with a carnal, claiming expression, he lowered his mouth to the inside of her thigh and kissed.

Martina gasped. The near intimacy made her feel incredibly vulnerable. "I...I..."

"Hang on," he said, and took her with his lips.

Flexing her fingers in his hair, she felt consumed and utterly possessed. His tongue laved the pearl of her femininity, creating a tender, delicious friction, sending her over the top once, then again.

Martina cried out, and Noah pulled back. He lowered his jeans, fully exposing his huge arousal and drawing her hand to touch him. She stroked his hard shaft and he closed his eyes as if torn between pleasure and pain.

Trembling, she pulled herself up and tentatively pressed her lips to him. She opened her mouth over him and tasted the heady flavor of his passion.

Noah swore under his breath. "Not this time. I want to be inside you," he muttered, and eased her back on the desk.

In one swift thrust, he took her, and Martina knew she would never be the same.

She awakened with a gasp and bolted upright. Her heart pounding, her body hot, she took deep breaths and tried to gather her composure. Her cotton gown rubbed against her sensitive nipples. She was aroused, Martina realized in surprise. She closed her eyes against the sensations. She had been dreaming about Noah, and the dream had felt an awful lot like the one time she and Noah had made love and forgotten about contraception. The time, she realized, that their baby had been conceived. She'd heard there was a thin line between dreams and memories.

She rubbed her cheeks in dismay. Martina had tried so hard to run from Noah. First in Chicago, then in her mind and heart. She had only succeeded in delaying the inevitable. Now he was walking in her dreams.

Martina stared at the Web page she was constructing on her computer screen and heard a knock at her door. Actually, banging was a better description.

"Surprise!" called the familiar voices of her brothers and their families.

Smiling, she clicked "save" and hurried to the front door. Her two brothers, their wives, and her niece and nephews stood on her front porch.

"Aunt Martina, we've got presents for the baby

in your tummy!'' yelled Sam, Tyler and Jill's newly adopted son.

Martina swung open the door and gave the little boy a hug. He had been one of Tyler's patients, and the way the three of them had become a family still moved her. ''Hurry up and bring them to me, so I can open them all.''

Sam looked at her with huge brown eyes. ''Why? Is the baby gonna pop out right now?''

Martina laughed and shook her head at Tyler and Jill. ''Not yet. I just love presents.''

She stood and hugged the rest of the crowd, amazed at the number of gifts. ''Y'all did too much. My goodness, what possessed you?''

Brock, her oldest brother, hauled in a bassinet. ''We kept hoping you would see reason and move back to the ranch with Felicity, Bree, Jacob and me.''

''Or in with Jill and me,'' Tyler said pointedly.

Martina sighed and her heart swelled with love for her brothers. ''I guess you two are never going to stop looking after me.''

Brock and Tyler glanced knowingly at each other, then back at her. ''No,'' they both said at once.

''You need a keeper,'' Brock said.

''And it takes both of us to do the job,'' Tyler added.

Unbidden tears filled her eyes, catching her off guard. She gave a muffled sound of dismay and swiped them away.

Tyler immediately looked concerned. "You're crying? You'd rather eat glass than cry. What's wrong? Is something wrong with you or the baby?"

"No, I'm fine. Darn pregnancy hormones," she said quickly. Martina felt a twinge of the old frustration she'd felt as long as she could remember. Her brothers still didn't believe she could take care of herself. Even though she was twenty-four, gainfully employed, single, pregnant... She sighed. The single and pregnant part probably hadn't helped her case.

She smiled and kissed each brother on the cheek. "I'm not going to argue with you today. I'm too delighted with your visit." She glanced at her nephew Jacob. "Is that a swing?"

"My idea," Bree, her niece, said. "I baby-sit for the Walters, and the only time their baby stops screaming is when I put her in the swing. I have to keep cranking theirs, but the one we got you has a setting for infinity. That means it never stops."

Martina had a fleeting frightening image of her baby spending the first year of his life in a swing. Her dismay must have shown.

Brock's wife, Felicity, laughed. She put her arm around Martina. "She's exaggerating. Mrs. Walters usually asks Bree to keep the baby during colic time."

"If you moved in with us, Aunt Martina, I could take care of your baby during colic time," Bree said, slyly glancing at her father.

Brock gave a wink of approval.

Although she smelled a conspiracy, Martina's heart swelled at the obvious love between Brock and his daughter. The closeness they shared was the exact opposite of what Martina and her father had shared, and she thanked the Lord her precious niece wouldn't spend her childhood trying to make her father love her.

"That's tempting," Martina said, giving Bree a quick squeeze. "Maybe you can come stay with me awhile after the baby is born."

"I will," Felicity offered.

"So will I," Jill said.

Brock and Tyler exchanged a look of dissatisfaction. "It's bad enough that you won't move in with us," Tyler said.

"Where you belong," Brock added meaningfully.

"Now you're going to make us live without our wives."

"Temporarily," Jill said, still a newlywed. She shot a flirty smile at Tyler. "The reunion could be enjoyable."

Tyler plastered a stern expression on his face. "There she goes doing that PR thing again, trying to tell me a sow's ear is a silk purse."

"It's like what she did with you," Martina said with mock innocence, referring to the advertising campaign Jill had used to help Tyler raise money for the new pediatric wing at his hospital. "Got a great photographer, featured you in fund-raising ads and turned you into the state's most wanted doctor."

He slid his arm around Jill. "That ad campaign turned out to be costly, since she paid for it by becoming my wife."

"Best thing I ever did," Jill said.

Martina could see the love flowing between Tyler and Jill and felt a twinge of envy. They were practically glowing with devotion. It was disgusting. "Stop. This is so sweet I could throw up. Neither of you look as if you're suffering. Let's all go into the den while I get a good look at all the goodies you brought me."

Martina served lemonade while her brothers assembled the swing, a bassinet and a changing table.

Her nephew Jacob presented her with a dozen pacifiers.

He had flourished under Felicity's care. Who would have thought a boy could become more of a man by getting a Manhattan heiress for a stepmother? Martina glanced at her well-dressed, warmhearted sister-in-law. Felicity had worked magic for everyone at the Logan ranch. Sighing, Martina supposed the Logans had been due a change of luck in the romance department, and she was glad love had found her brothers, even if it hadn't found her.

"Thank you," she said to Jacob, bewildered by the variety of pacifiers. "But why so many?"

He shrugged and hooked his thumbs in his belt loops. "Bree said babies don't always like the first pacifier, so I thought I'd give the baby a choice just in case he hollers like Dad says I did when I was little.''

Martina's lips twitched. "Babies don't cry *all* the time."

"I know," he said. "They sleep and poop, too. That's why we filled up the back seat with diapers. I'll bring 'em in."

Martina opened her mouth to respond, but the doorbell rang, interrupting her. She walked to the front door and opened it to a man dressed in a mechanic's uniform. "I'm Jimmy Steen with Lone Star Auto Service Center, and I'm here to check a car that belongs to Martina Logan."

Hearing her brothers approach behind her, she shook her head. "Why? I haven't had any problems."

"We got a call from—" he pulled a folded paper from his pocket "—Coltrane," he said. "Noah Coltrane called and asked us to make sure your vehicle is in perfect running condition."

"Coltrane," Brock ominously echoed behind her. "I thought he was staying away from you."

"He better be staying away from you," Tyler said.

Martina's stomach twisted. "This isn't a good time," she said to the mechanic and turned to face her brothers. Even though they had almost suffocated her by overprotecting her, Martina loved Brock and Tyler with all her heart. Brock still wore a scar on his cheek from rescuing her from an unbroken horse when she was a toddler. Tyler had done things for her most brothers wouldn't dream of, such as painting her nails and braiding her hair. They had tried to make up for her father's lack of attention and love.

This was why she and Noah could never be together. This and the fact that Noah wasn't truly in love with her.

She swallowed over a tight feeling in her throat. "Noah found me," she said quietly. "He knows I'm having his baby."

Tyler's jaw hardened. "He hasn't tried to hurt you in any way, has he?"

"No, not at all." She bit her lip. "He, uh, wanted me to marry him, but of course I said no."

"Of course," Brock said. "He should know better. You'd never marry a good-for-nothing Coltrane."

Felicity joined them, catching Martina's gaze. "He might not be totally good-for-nothing," she said. "After all, Martina must have seen something in him."

"That was a fling," Tyler said.

"A big mistake," Brock said. "She was vulnerable and homesick and he took advantage of her."

Felicity raised a fine eyebrow. "You could be underestimating both Martina and Noah."

"I *know* Noah Coltrane," Tyler said. "I traded punches with him throughout high school."

Felicity bristled. "I'm a little sensitive to the idea

that zebras don't change their stripes, because I did. Are you the same person you were in high school?''

''No, but…'' Brock narrowed his eyes. ''Why are you taking up for Noah? You know the problems the Coltranes have caused.''

The possibility of her brother and sister-in-law fighting filled Martina with distress. ''This isn't necessary,'' she began.

Felicity locked gazes with her husband. ''Circumstances are different now. We have to think about what's best for Martina and her baby.''

''That doesn't include Noah Coltrane,'' Brock returned.

''That's not for you to decide.''

''Please stop,'' Martina said, feeling close to tears. ''If ever a man didn't need someone to defend him, it's Noah. He's quite capable of defending himself. And this discussion is moot because the stars will have to fall on Texas before Noah and I get married.''

Both of her brothers visibly relaxed, but Felicity still wore a look of concern. ''Jacob tells me you brought me diapers,'' Martina said to her. ''Why don't you bring them in while I go up to the nursery?''

Martina walked to the nursery and tried to gather her wits. The one thing she hated most about pregnancy was this completely foreign but overwhelming urge to cry. Feeling pulled in opposite directions at once, she bit her lip to get her emotions under control.

"Martina," Felicity said from the doorway.

Martina stiffened her backbone and turned to find both sisters-in-law watching her. "You really don't need to defend Noah."

"I've talked with him," Felicity said.

Martina gaped at her and lifted her shoulders in confusion. "How? When?"

"I ran into him at the bookstore one day. Actually, he saw me and remembered me from the wedding. He asked me to have coffee with him. He was so polite and so hungry for information about you that I couldn't refuse. I felt guilty afterward, but Brock and Tyler are so unreasonable about the Coltranes."

"I second that," Jill said.

Martina felt confused and exposed. "What did he ask you?"

"Little things. Your favorite food and color. Between you and Brock, I've gathered enough about you that I could answer most of his questions. I told him if he hurt you I would cut out his heart. His reply is what made me think that everyone needs to give Noah Coltrane a chance."

Martina almost didn't want to hear what Noah had said. She was having a difficult time holding fast to her determination to keep him at arm's length.

"What did he say?" Jill asked.

"He said if he hurt you, he would supply me with the sword."

A chill ran through Martina.

"I know what it's like to be underestimated. I think you do too," Felicity said. "Don't underestimate Noah. Do what is best for you."

"I am. Noah doesn't really love me," she said, forcing the words from her mouth as much for herself as for Jill and Felicity. "This is some kind of male, family-honor thing for him."

Jill looked undecided. "We just want you to know we're here for you whatever you choose to do." She brushed her hands together as if dispensing with the conversational topic. "Speaking of choices, what would you like to do now?"

Sit down and cry, Martina wanted to say. Instead, she swallowed her emotions and said, "I'd like to decide where to put everything you brought." She pretended to focus on the task at hand, but in her mind, she felt Noah's presence. The strange connection she'd felt with him in Chicago and buried when she'd left wrapped around her like a silken rope. Soft but deceptively strong. Felicity and Brock's argument played through her mind in stereo, however, reminding her that she couldn't give in to crazy fantasies about Noah.

For her family. For herself.

Six

Martina glanced at her cuckoo clock for the fortieth time and scowled. She was getting used to his calls and his visits. When he'd called last night, he'd told her he would see her tonight around seven. It was after eight. What if he'd been in an accident? Her heart stuttered at the thought. Had he forgotten? She struggled with pure liquid fury.

She'd been reviewing the same part of a Web page for the past thirty minutes. She shouldn't care. It shouldn't matter. In fact, she should be relieved. After all, Noah had become an unwelcome intruder in her life.

The doorbell rang and she sprang from her chair

and ran to open the front door. "Where in hell have you been?" she asked, searching Noah's face. "You look tired."

"A tractor-trailer turned over on the highway, spilled oil over the road. I had to take a detour."

"Oh," Martina said, and took a careful breath. "Did you forget your cell phone?"

He rubbed the back of his neck. "I tried a couple of times, but I must've been in a dead zone." He met her gaze. "Are you pissed off or upset?"

Martina felt a surge of conflicting emotions and the terrible, overwhelming urge to cry. "Oh, damn," she muttered. "Damn. Absolutely not," she sternly told herself.

"Huh?" Noah reached out to lift her chin so he could see her face. "Are you okay?"

"I'm not," she insisted.

His brow wrinkled. "Then what's wrong?"

Martina shook her head and took several quick breaths. "I'm fine. I'm not going to cry."

He looked at her in shock. "Cry?"

"I'm not going to cry," she said, closing her eyes and feeling a tiny tear escape the corner of one.

She felt his warm, long finger on her cheek. "You were worried about me," he said in astonishment. "You're upset because you didn't want anything to happen to me."

Martina opened her eyes. "Don't read anything into it. It doesn't mean anything," she told him. "It's those dingdong pregnancy hormones."

He pulled her against him. "You missed me."

"I did not," Martina said, relishing the comfort of his arms.

"Okay, then I'll leave."

She tightened her hands on his arms. "Don't," she whispered, a request she couldn't stifle.

"Admit it," he said. "You care for me."

"I care for every human being on the planet except ax murderers and very mean people."

"But you didn't worry about every human being on the planet tonight. You worried about me." He lowered his head putting his mouth inches from hers. "Admit it."

You can't make me. You can't make me, she thought, zipping her lips.

"Shy?" Noah asked in a gently mocking voice. "I'm surprised. You're many things, but I've never thought of you as shy."

"I'm not!" Completely out of sorts, she felt as if her composure had taken the last train to Beaumont.

Startling her, he swung her up into his arms and carried her into the softly lit den. "What are you doing?" she exclaimed. "Trying to give yourself a hernia?"

"There you go again—worrying about me. Careful, Martina, or I'll start thinking you truly care about me."

"Oh, that's ridiculous," she muttered, relieved when he set her down on the couch. She started to rise, but Noah put his hands on either side of her, trapping her.

"I would be just fine if you would give me a little space," she told him.

"Maybe later," he said, pulling her into his arms and lowering his head.

He took her mouth, and Martina's composure left Beaumont and headed for Mexico. He kissed her intently, as if to reassure her that he was very much alive. His mouth, a seductive combination of supple and soft, nibbled at hers, sucking her lips, and his tongue slid over hers.

The low, sexual murmur rising from his throat lit a hidden flame inside her. She could almost believe he wanted her. His breath and hers mingled, her heart pounded, and he continued to kiss her.

One of his hands wandered to her tank top, lifting it, and his slightly callused palm touched her bare belly. His fingers caressed her while his mouth grew hungrier with each passing moment.

Martina's temperature shot to sweltering, and she felt her breasts throb with need. As if he knew the way her blood flowed through her body, Noah skimmed his fingers upward to the underside of her breasts. Lifting her bra, he rubbed his thumb over one breast, getting close to, but not quite touching, her nipple.

Unchecked desire licked through her, and she suckled his tongue, craving the way he made her feel. His thumb glanced over her nipple, and she shuddered.

"Like that?" he asked in a taunting sexual voice against her lips. Giving her no opportunity to answer, he took her mouth again and began to rub her turgid nipple between his thumb and forefinger.

The caress tightened her nether regions with shocking speed and force.

"Oh." The helpless sound escaped her mouth.

"You feel incredible," he told her, lifting his other hand to her other breast, stroking and teasing her.

Martina felt as if he was stimulating her intimately. Each tug of his fingers on her nipples squeezed a coil deep inside her. Unable to remain still, she undulated against him.

He groaned and lowered his hand, replacing his fingers with his warm, wet mouth. The sight of his dark head against her pale breast was too erotic to bear. Closing her eyes, she fought the escalating pleasure. This couldn't be happening, she thought.

Noah's tongue cupped her nipple, sucking, sending her over the top and crying out. A shocking, intense climax rocked through her. "Oh, my!"

She bit her lip as his terrible, wonderful mouth continued, sending her into another spasm of pleasure. Helpless and vulnerable, Martina felt a well of emotion that swelled in her eyes.

"Oh, damn, not again," she whispered, distressed.

Noah pulled back and looked into her eyes. She looked away, swiping at hers.

"Come here," he said, pulling her into his arms.

"This is crazy," she wailed. "How do you..." She broke off, feeling a fresh threat of tears. "This is insane. We're wrong for each other. You don't really want me. You want the baby and your honor and—"

Noah moved her hand to his very hard masculinity, abruptly cutting her off. She savored the intimacy of touching him for a few seconds. She savored the hope that he truly did want her for a few seconds. Then the baby kicked and so did reality.

Martina drew back. "You can't want me."

His eyes dark with desire and challenge, he nudged her gaze upward to meet his. "Why not?"

"Because I'm very big," she said.

"With my baby," he said, rubbing his hands over her full abdomen. He lowered his mouth to kiss the bare skin. "This makes you the sexiest woman in the world to me."

Martina searched her brain for a response, but found none. He almost made her believe it. Almost.

"I want to make love to you."

Panic shot through her. "Oh, no." She pulled back and shook her head. "Not a good idea."

"Why?" he asked, his slight grin belying the serious glint in his eye. "It's not like you'll get pregnant."

"It's just not a good idea."

"You really have no idea how sexy you are to me right now. Your body is so responsive, your breasts full. Do you have any idea how much of a turn-on it is knowing I can bring you to climax just by touching your breasts? Imagine what else could happen if—?"

"—I had no idea I would." Martina shook her head adamantly. She didn't need to imagine. Reality was clouding her head enough.

"Never before?" he asked.

"No," Martina said, feeling her cheeks heat self-consciously. "I think I may have seen something about it in one of the pregnancy books I read."

"Really! What did it say?"

"I don't remember much. I think I skimmed that part, but the point is—"

"What *do* you remember?"

Martina sighed, wishing she could transport herself to Anywhere-elseville. "It just said something about how women's breasts are sometimes more sensitive during pregnancy and some women have been known to have orgasms just by…" *Help!*

"By touching," he finished. "With hands or mouth."

Martina felt his words like a touch and her body remembered his recent caresses. She shook her head. "This is crazy. You've got to stop."

"Why?" he asked in an irritatingly calm voice.

"Because we're not right for each other, and—"

"Why?" he asked again.

"Well, there's the fact that your family hates mine and mine hates yours."

"But I don't hate you, and you don't hate me," he said. "So why are we not right for each other? What don't you like about me?"

Martina blinked. He'd taken her off guard again.

"You don't like the way I look?"

Her gaze helplessly fell over his strong body and chiseled facial features. "I, uh…" She swallowed. "I don't not like the way you look."

His lips twitched at her grudging response, but he continued. "Do I not turn you on sexually?"

She cleared her throat. She couldn't very well deny he turned her on after the way she'd just responded to him. "I, uh…" She exhaled in frustration. "Yes, of course you turn me on. I don't think I'd be pregnant if you didn't."

He nodded. "Then it must be my personality, the way I think and act."

Unable to bear the riot her emotions were causing inside her, Martina stood. "No, I like…" She trailed off, confused and frustrated. Noah's personality was what never failed to bowl her over, but she couldn't tell him that. "Yes, that's it. You're just too damn smart," she said angrily. "And intuitive. You're too intuitive. And you argue with me too much."

Noah stood. "You would have no use for a man who didn't meet you head-to-head and toe-to-toe. You're too strong a woman not to demand strength in your man."

Frustration roared through her and another spate of tears threatened. Martina bit her lip, refusing to cry. Heaven help her, this man knew her better than she'd realized. What in hell was she going to do?

He gave her an assessing gaze. "You look like you could use some time to yourself."

He was right. And wrong. But she latched on to the offer. "Yes, thank you."

"Anything else?" he asked.

"Anything else what?" she asked, still confused.

"Is there anything else you need?"

Martina refused to think about what he said anymore. If she did, she feared her brain would explode. "Cheesecake," she said. "I need cheesecake."

He gave her an odd look, then shrugged. "Okay. I brought something for the baby, but I left it in the truck. I'll be back in a minute."

Curious but wary, Martina followed him to the door.

Remaining on the porch, he opened the door and gave her a CD. "It's Mozart," he said. "There've been studies done that suggest listening to Mozart can increase a child's intelligence."

Touched, Martina scanned the CD. He was thinking about the baby even when he wasn't here with her.

"I don't want to try to make Super Baby, but if a little music will make life nicer for her..." He shrugged.

"Him," Martina corrected.

"We'll see," he said with a knowing grin. "G'night. I'll call you."

"G'night," Martina echoed, and fought a hint of a bereft feeling as she watched him leave. Closing the door and locking it, she opened the CD and put it on, allowing the music to wash over her. Too restless for sleep and leery of the dreams she might have, she poured herself some fruit juice and returned to her computer. She needed to lose herself in her work. She needed to lose herself in something besides Noah.

Mozart played and moments passed. The doorbell rang, surprising her, dragging her from her work. She eyed the clock and wondered who could be at her door. Staring outside her peephole, she saw no one, but heard the sound of a car engine. She checked the peephole again and saw no one.

Irritated, she opened the door and saw a vehicle disappear around the corner. She frowned, wondering if the ringing doorbell had been a product of her imagination. She happened to glance down and spotted a brown paper bag.

Picking it up, Martina peeked inside.

A slice of cheesecake.

Her heart turned over. *Damn him. Damn him. Damn him.*

He was getting to her. Satisfaction pumped through Noah at the thought as he drove to the Coltrane ranch. Martina was starting to face the fact that she wasn't immune to him. Soon she would face the fact that they should marry.

Noah wasn't worried about love. Their passion and their child was enough to bind them to each other. He didn't want love clouding the more important need for them to get married.

Noah had always doubted that romantic love was in the cards for him. His mentor, Zachary, had always stressed how important it was for a man to find his purpose and perform it. Noah had quickly learned his purpose was to bring innovations to the Coltrane ranch to increase revenue and secure his and his brothers' future. In the back of his mind, he'd vaguely believed he was securing the future of the next generation of Coltranes. That belief was no longer vague. It held a distinct picture in his mind of Martina and his child.

His purpose, also, was to bring honor and integrity to the Coltrane name. God knows, after his father's reputation, the Coltranes needed every drop of honor they could produce. He felt a sliver of discomfort. In that respect, Martina was correct. He had a passion for her, but the bottom line was that this was a matter of honor. She would eventually adjust to that fact, he was certain.

Turning in to the long drive to the house, Noah relished his progress. Soon, Martina would be where she belonged. With him. He tried looking at the ranch through her eyes. Since she had grown up on a ranch, many of the sights, sounds and smells would be familiar. The flat Texas terrain and the dry heat would come as no surprise.

He pulled his truck to a stop and glanced at the large two-story wood-frame house that stood like a stubborn weed on dry rocky ground. Although the Coltrane home showed little in the way of feminine influence, it was freshly painted and renovated, and boasted most modern conveniences.

Mounting the steps, he thought Martina would approve of the rebuilt porch and refinished oak floors. He walked through the downstairs, taking inventory. She might want to add some rugs or pictures, he thought, looking at the clean bare walls, but she would like the modern appliances in the kitchen. She might want to add some lamps. Sometimes the rooms seemed dark. He would clear out a room for her to do her Web page design. With a few minor changes, he decided she would adjust. She would like it, he thought, following the sound of his brothers in the TV room. No problem—

Noah stopped short at the sight that greeted him. Adam and Gideon lay sprawled on the sofa and recliner in their boxers. With a book propped in his lap, Adam chugged a beer and Gideon sucked on a cigar, his newsmagazine abandoned on the floor beside him.

Wearing headphones, Jonathan sat on the floor watching television while he hummed off-key.

"Be quiet," Gideon said.

"He can't hear you," Adam said, and turned up the volume on the wrestling show.

No-woman's-land.

Gideon glanced up. "Yo, brother, how goes the taming of the shrew?"

Noah sighed and raked his hand through his hair. "Progressing," he said, and sat down on the sofa. He stared unseeingly at the television screen, his mind busy.

"No bite or claw marks?" Gideon asked with a smart-aleck grin.

Noah shook his head.

"What are you doing to cut down on the battle scars?"

"I feed her," Noah said, his lips twitching as he imagined Martina's enjoyment of the cheesecake he'd left her.

Still wearing headphones, Jonathan glanced up at him and nodded, yelling, "Hi."

Noah pulled back one of the earphones. "I gave her the Mozart CD for the baby."

"What'd she think?" Jonathan asked.

"I don't know, but she didn't look like she wanted to slap me. That's an improvement."

"Any chance there'll be a wedding soon?"

Noah felt a burning determination. "Damn straight." He looked at his oldest brother, who he'd noticed hadn't said anything. "Talk," Noah said to him. "Front porch."

Adam glanced at him and slowly rose from his

easy chair. "Okay." Setting Homer's *Odyssey* aside, Adam joined Noah on the front porch. In his boxers, he was an incongruous picture of a "good ol' boy" traditional cattleman with a closet appreciation for literary classics.

"What do you want now?" he asked, as he had asked Noah dozens of times before. Although Adam gave the impression of being reluctant to change, he offered a steadiness that had provided a balance to him and his brothers.

"When I walked into the house tonight, it occurred to me that a woman considering moving into our home might find the prospect difficult."

Adam propped his beer on the porch rail and glanced down at his skimpy attire. His mouth quirked in an ironic grin. "I don't know why."

"Oh, something about the combination of the *World of Wrestling* full blast on the TV, men sitting in their underwear drinking beer, smoking cigars and yelling at each other."

Adam shook his head. "You're gonna have a hard time changing our habits."

"I'm not planning on it."

Adam took another drink of beer. "Then what?"

"You know that building we've been putting together for offices?"

"Yeah."

"I was thinking about using some of my own money and making it into a house, instead."

Adam let out a long breath. "Has she agreed to marry you?"

"No, but—"

"Don't you think you're gambling against the house? You keep forgetting her family hates us."

"I haven't forgotten it," Noah said. The reality of the grudge burned like a hot poker in his gut every waking minute. "But Martina is going to marry me."

"She and her brothers just don't know it yet, right?"

Noah appealed to his brother's sense of the bottom line. "I'll take it out of my own pocket," he said. "I've done pretty well with some of my day trading."

Adam scratched his head and shot him a glance mingled with doubt and respect. "Good luck. You're gonna need it."

Seven

A ringing sound jerked Martina from her sleep. Disoriented, she sat up in bed. The ringing continued and she shook her head, trying to clear it. When she realized the sound was coming from the phone, a dozen thoughts flew through her mind.

If this was Noah, she was going to give that man a piece of her mind. He hadn't just been late this time. He hadn't shown up at all. She'd paced the house the entire evening watching the clock and then had a difficult time going to sleep.

What if it was someone else, though? Brock? Tyler?

She reached across the bed and snatched the phone from the cradle. "Hello?"

PLAY

RUN
FOR THE
ROSES

and get

THREE FREE GIFTS!

HOW TO PLAY:

1. With a coin, carefully scratch off the silver box at the right. Then check the claim chart to see what we have for you — **2 FREE BOOKS** and a **FREE GIFT** — **ALL YOURS FREE!**

2. Send back the card and you'll receive two brand-new Silhouette Desire® novels. These books have a cover price of $3.99 each in the U.S. and $4.50 each in Canada, but they are yours to keep absolutely free.

3. There's no catch. You're under no obligation to buy anything. We charge nothing — ZERO — for your first shipment. And you don't have to make any minimum number of purchases — not even one!

4. The fact is, thousands of readers enjoy receiving books by mail from the Silhouette Reader Service™. They enjoy the convenience of home delivery...they like getting the best new novels at discount prices, BEFORE they're available in stores... and they love their *Heart to Heart* subscriber newsletter featuring author news, horoscopes, recipes, book reviews and much more!

5. We hope that after receiving your free books you'll want to remain a subscriber. But the choice is yours — to continue or cancel, any time at all! So why not take us up on our invitation, with no risk of any kind. You'll be glad you did!

Visit us online at
www.eHarlequin.com

This surprise mystery gift
Could be yours **FREE** –
When you play
RUN for the ROSES

DETACH AND MAIL CARD TODAY!

The Silhouette Reader Service™ — Here's how it works:

Accepting your 2 free books and gift places you under no obligation to buy anything. You may keep the books and gift and return the shipping statement marked "cancel." If you do not cancel, about a month later we'll send you 6 additional novels and bill you just $3.34 each in the U.S., or $3.74 each in Canada, plus 25¢ delivery per book and applicable taxes if any.* That's the complete price and — compared to cover prices of $3.99 each in the U.S. and $4.50 each in Canada — it's quite a bargain! You may cancel at any time, but if you choose to continue, every month we'll send you 6 more books, which you may either purchase at the discount price or return to us and cancel your subscription.

*Terms and prices subject to change without notice. Sales tax applicable in N.Y. Canadian residents will be charged applicable provincial taxes and GST.

If offer card is missing write to: Silhouette Reader Service, 3010 Walden Ave., P.O. Box 1867, Buffalo NY 14240-1867

BUSINESS REPLY MAIL
FIRST-CLASS MAIL   PERMIT NO. 717   BUFFALO, NY

POSTAGE WILL BE PAID BY ADDRESSEE

SILHOUETTE READER SERVICE
3010 WALDEN AVE
PO BOX 1867
BUFFALO NY 14240-9952

NO POSTAGE
NECESSARY
IF MAILED
IN THE
UNITED STATES

"Martina Logan?" a male voice said.

"Yes."

"Sorry to call so late. This is Jonathan Coltrane. Noah won't be able to make it tonight."

Martina glanced at the fluorescent-blue numbers on her alarm clock. "Since it's after 2 a.m., that thought had occurred to me."

"Yeah, well, he was in an accident on his way to see you. The doctor says he's gonna be okay, but—"

Martina's heart sank to her knees. "Doctor?"

"Yeah, the ambulance took him to the hospital. His truck is totaled. He's gonna be real pissed off."

Martina swallowed over her racing panic. "How is he?"

"Broken ribs, punctured lung, concussion and one of his legs is bruised pretty bad. He'll be sore and cranky the next few days."

Wide awake now, she clenched her hands to keep them from trembling. "Which hospital is he in?"

"County Hospital. We'll bring him home in the morning. The doctor would've let him go except for the punctured lung and the concussion. They wake him every so often and ask his name. I was in there one of the times they woke him, and he muttered something about needing to call you right before he fell asleep again."

"Thank you for telling me," Martina said, her mind whirling.

"You're welcome," Jonathan said. "G'night."

He hung up and Martina listened to the dial tone for a full minute before she returned the phone to the cradle. What if Noah had been hurt worse? A chill ran through her. What if he had died? For a moment, the darkness felt as if it had closed in around her, suffocating her.

Throwing back the covers, she rose from the bed and flipped on one light, then another and another. She walked to the hall and turned on that light, followed the steps downstairs and turned on nearly every light until the house was bright enough for Christmas.

"It's not as if I'll be going back to sleep anytime soon," she murmured to herself, and tried to deal with the terrible fear and pain she felt at the thought of Noah being hurt or dying.

Pacing into the kitchen, she poured herself some orange juice and gulped it. Lately, it seemed as if she was always thirsty. She kept picturing Noah in his truck and the crashing, grinding sound of metal. In her mind, she saw him against white sheets in the hospital. Another more insidious image flashed of Noah dead.

Her heart raced double time and panic coursed through her. She didn't want her baby growing up without Noah. For all her uncertainties about him, she believed he would be a wonderful father, a far different father than the one she had experienced. Noah would not ignore his child. Although Martina tried not to focus on it, when her mother died she might as well have been orphaned. If not for her brothers, she wouldn't have experienced any love as a child.

The thought tore at her, tugging fiercely at her sense of loyalty, as it always did. Martina closed her eyes and shook her head. She couldn't deal with that right now. Right now, she had the edgy, overpowering need to see that Noah was all right.

Noah awoke to the sound of loud voices outside his hospital room and winced at the pain in his chest. At the moment, it hurt to breathe. The only thing he wanted was blessed sleep. If that nurse poked him and asked his name one more time, he was going to tell her he was an alien. Or the president. Or, he thought with a pained grin, a woman. Maybe that one from the Zorro movie. Martina looked a lot like her.

"If you're not related to Mr. Coltrane, I can't allow you in," the nurse said firmly.

Noah opened his eyes at the mention of his name. His gaze encountered Jonathan and Gideon.

"What?" Gideon rose and cracked the door.

"This is ridiculous. All I want to do is see Noah. I have no interest in even talking to him." Martina's voice carried into Noah's room.

Gideon turned an accusing gaze on Jonathan. "There is one very pregnant, very upset woman out there. Why in hell did you call her? Adam said we shouldn't."

Jonathan shrugged. "Adam left."

"He's gonna fry your butt."

"Not if he doesn't find out," Jonathan returned. "Not unless the baby of the family snitches on me."

Gideon scowled. "You son of a—"

"Would you two shut up so I can hear Martina?" Noah demanded. "I want to hear this."

"What is so—" Gideon began.

"Shut up," Jonathan and Noah said in unison.

"You haven't given me an acceptable reason to allow you into Mr. Coltrane's room. This patient has experienced head trauma and shouldn't be disturbed."

"This is not the first time Mr. Coltrane has acted as if he has experienced head trauma, but that's another matter," Martina said. "Mr. Coltrane is…"

"She's not going to be able to say it." Noah shook his head, then winced at the pain.

"Say what?" Gideon asked in exasperation.

"You'll hear."

"He contributed genetic material," Martina said.

"Pardon?" the nurse said.

"He supplied necessary chromosomes," Martina continued.

"A sperm donor!" the nurse exclaimed. "You think I should let you in there because he was your sperm donor?"

"He was not my sperm donor," Martina hotly denied. "Noah Coltrane donated his sperm the old-fashioned way, I'm expecting his child, and he has asked me to marry him.''

Noah started to chuckle, but it hurt too much.

''Oh, you're his fiancée,'' the nurse said. ''Why didn't you say so? You can go in.''

''Thank you,'' Martina said in a cool voice, then muttered, pushing open Noah's door, ''that's right. I did not say I was his fiancée.''

''I'm asleep,'' Noah whispered to his brothers and closed his eyes.

At her entrance, Noah heard both his brothers rise to their feet. Not surprised she had that effect on him, he thought. She'd probably made more than one man think about kneeling.

He smelled her sweet scent and felt her gaze as she paused for a long moment at his bedside. He was struck by an overpowering urge to see her, and it took surprising willpower to keep his eyes closed.

''Is he really okay?'' she whispered.

''Yeah,'' Jonathan said. ''He's just—''

''—sleeping,'' Gideon finished.

''Which of you is Jonathan?'' she asked, her voice like honey over his pain.

''I am,'' Jonathan said. ''You didn't have to come.''

''Yes, I did. I, uh…'' She cleared her throat. ''I needed to see for myself that he was okay.''

Her simple statement soothed his jangled nerve endings and abused body. Her presence both stimulated and relaxed him, and he felt himself drifting again. Martina was here and she cared. Everything wasn't all right, but it was a damn sight better than it had been.

The next time Noah awakened, it was to an empty room, and he wondered if he had dreamed her into his room, wished her there in his state of concussion.

His door whooshed open and Martina appeared with a cup of coffee in her hand. Her gaze met his. "You're awake," she said.

"Yeah."

"How are you feeling?"

"Okay," he automatically responded, busy drinking in the sight of her.

"Okay," she echoed in disbelief.

"Well, as long as I don't breathe or move, I feel okay."

She smiled at his light response, then her expression shifted. If he didn't know better, he would say she looked worried.

"I'm sorry about the accident," she said.

"Yeah, the truck's a goner."

"I wasn't talking about the truck," she said. "I was talking about you."

A tiny drop of hope trickled through his blood. "You didn't want me to croak?" he asked.

"No. I didn't."

"You might miss me," he said.

"The baby would miss having a pretty wonderful father."

Life wasn't worth living if a man didn't push his

luck every now and then, Noah thought, so he pushed. "Then maybe you should marry me like you told the nurse you would."

Martina stopped and stared at him for a full moment. "You heard that?"

"Most of it," he said.

"But you were asleep," she said, distress creeping into her voice.

"Well, after you whispered with my brothers, I fell asleep, but—"

Her eyes lit with anger. "You eavesdropped and pretended you were asleep. What a slimy—"

"Just a minute, Princess Logan." Noah held up his hand and winced at the pain. "You were practically having a catfight with the nurse right outside my room. That's not eavesdropping."

"But you pretended—"

"Not for long. With the way I've felt since my truck rolled, I'd rather sleep through the next few days than win the lottery."

Her skin paled. "It rolled? Your truck rolled?"

Reluctant to alarm her, he bit back an oath. "It was just a little roll."

Martina sank onto the corner of his bed. "There's no such thing as a little roll. Your brothers hedged on the severity of the accident."

"They were just following instincts. Good instincts," he said. "No need to unnecessarily alarm a pregnant woman."

"I don't need to be protected."

"Yeah, you do," Noah said. "It's okay. This is one of the times in your life you need to be protected. You can't run as fast as usual. You can't lift as much as usual, although I suspect you try," he added with a frown. "You need to be protected, and it's okay. It won't always be that way. It doesn't mean you're not as strong. It just means your body is busy doing something else at the moment. It's busy getting our baby ready for the big entrance."

She looked at him and he could see she half-agreed and half-disagreed. Her eyes rounded slightly and she put her hand on her belly. "Sometimes I wonder if he already knows."

"Knows what?" Noah prompted.

Reluctance shimmered in her vibrant blue eyes. She hesitated. "Sometimes I wonder if the baby already knows your voice."

Noah's gut tightened. "Is the baby moving right now?"

Martina nodded, paused a few seconds, then moved closer to him. She put his hand on her abdomen, and Noah immediately felt a jab and a kick. He met Martina's gaze and saw the wonder in her eyes, the same wonder that burst inside him. The moment was a magical sliver of time. "Amazing," he said, lacing his fingers through hers over her abdomen.

He watched Martina look at their intertwined hands. She bit her lip and eased backward.

Her retreat annoyed him. His patience had been

stretched to the limit. He wanted her to admit that she belonged with him. He wanted her to agree to marry him so they could raise the baby together. He wanted to throw her doubt, uncertainty and torn loyalties into a bottomless pit, and then throw her over his shoulder and take her home.

He felt a dull throb in his chest, leg and head, and reluctantly admitted he probably wasn't in the best shape for hauling anybody over his shoulder. He deliberately tamped down his impatience. "Where are my brothers?"

"They went home," she said. "They said—"

The door swung open and the doctor appeared. He flipped through the chart. "I see you made it through the night without too much trouble," he said. "Although the nurse said you objected to the frequent checks."

"She objected to the idea of me throwing a bedpan at her if she woke me once more before 5 a.m.," Noah said.

The doctor put his stethoscope to Noah's chest. "Breathe normally," he said, then put the stethoscope to his back. "Again.

"Rest for the next few days. You can sit up, but no physical exertion until your lung and ribs begin to heal. I suspect you won't feel like doing much, anyway. Plenty of fluids." He nodded in Martina's direction. "He's all yours, Mrs. Coltrane."

Martina's eyes rounded. She opened her mouth.

"Thank you very much," Noah said before she could voice her denial.

The doctor left the room and Noah reached for the telephone. "I need to call one of my brothers to pick me up."

Martina put her hand over his, preventing him from picking it up. "That's not necessary. I'm taking you to the ranch," she said.

Surprised, he raised his eyebrows. "Really?"

Her eyes flickered with brief uncertainty, but she took a breath and seemed to gird herself with determination. "I'm going to stay," she said. "For just a few days," she emphasized.

He opened his mouth to tell her he wasn't that hurt, that he didn't need her to care for him, but the notion of Martina at the Coltrane ranch was so tempting it made his mouth water.

"I feel somewhat responsible for your accident," she said. "After all, you were coming to see me when it happened."

"You aren't responsible. It could have happened to me anytime. You can't predict when another truck driver has had too much to drink and his vehicle goes out of control and strikes yours."

"I can accept that mentally," she said, lacing her hands together. "But…"

"But?" he prompted.

"But I just feel responsible. Your brothers are busy and you will need someone to help you for the next few days. It feels right that I should do it."

Noah wished like hell that it would feel right to Martina to be with him because that was where she belonged. He could push her to confess deeper feelings for him, he thought. Another time, he promised himself he would. He stifled a sigh. "So this is about your honor," Noah said slowly.

She met his gaze, then looked downward. "I suppose you could say that."

"Honor's not bad. It's not a bad place to start at all."

She met his gaze again and lifted her chin, the emotion in her blue eyes inscrutable. "For some things."

Noah was still sleeping when Martina pulled into the Coltrane driveway. She felt uneasy. This land had been forbidden to her since before she was born, and it felt very uncomfortable not only to drive on it, but also to know she would be here for the next few days. If her brothers found out... Her stomach plunged. She slammed the door on those thoughts.

She took in the lay of the land and decided something about the Coltrane ranch seemed more primitive to her. Perhaps it was the buildings under construction, or the fact that no white fence or bluebonnets lined the drive.

Or perhaps it was the house, she thought, as she slowed to view it. Painted brown with no shutters and no vegetation surrounding it, the house reminded her of a barn without the warmth.

She slid a glance at Noah. He must have noticed the difference in speed, for he shifted. Despite his denial, she was sure he felt terrible. His color was off, and dark circles rimmed his eyes. Beneath his denim shirt, she knew his chest was taped. Given Noah's mile-wide macho streak, he would probably forbid her to help him up the front steps. Martina decided to leave the car running while she enlisted the help of one of his brothers.

As she opened the car door and eased out, then headed for the house, it occurred to her that no Logan had ever set foot on Coltrane land without being armed. She lifted her chin and firmly pressed the doorbell.

A tall, unsmiling, unfriendly-looking man opened the door and looked at her suspiciously. This must be Adam, the oldest Coltrane brother, she concluded. She hadn't met him at the hospital. Martina felt the power of generations of distrust flow between them. Her unease grew.

Stiffening her back, she reminded herself that she was armed. Inside the small purse slung on her shoulder was a tiny silk envelope of something that gave her courage. Her secret talisman. Oh, yes, Martina was armed. With baby booties.

Eight

"I brought Noah home from the hospital and I know he's going to try to overdo, so I need someone to help him up the stairs."

Adam Coltrane looked at her as if she were an alien, which, in a way, she was.

She heard the scrape of Noah's boots on the steps behind her. "I'm fine on my own."

She rolled her eyes. "And he complains about my independence."

"I can handle him from here," Adam said. "Thanks for giving him a ride."

"She's staying," Noah said.

Adam's face froze. "She's what?"

"Just for a few days," Martina assured him. "Believe me, I'm just as uncomfortable with this as you are, but Noah will need some extra help the next few days, and it's not fair for you or your brothers to tend to him when the reason Noah crashed was because he was coming to see me."

She felt Noah's hand at her back. "You look terrible. You need to lie down," she said.

"Thank you," Noah said in dry tone. "You're not going to turn into a fussy, demanding woman who tries to order me around, are you?"

Martina smiled brightly. "Of course not. I'll be an assertive woman who reminds you of the things you need to do to heal quickly. The quicker you heal," she said, "the quicker I leave."

"No need to rush," he said in a voice that made her nerve endings ripple with sensual possibilities. "If someone lies down with me, maybe I'll rest better."

Martina felt a rush of warmth and a tinge of embarrassment, but she refused to show either. "Then we'll have to see if we can round up a teddy bear for you."

Noah chuckled, then winced and grabbed his ribs. "Oh, Lord, if you have any pity, don't make me laugh."

"Then don't try to seduce me when you can't do anything about it," Martina said as gently as she could.

"Sweetheart," Noah said with a dangerous light

in his eyes, "don't say I can't. That's like waving a red flag."

Martina struggled with the awareness that always seemed to shimmer between them. "I definitely don't want to bring out the bull in you," she murmured, then turned to Adam. "I think we need to get him into bed. Will you help?"

Adam blinked, his eyes still wary.

Martina's impatience climbed up the scale. "So what are you worried about? That I'll knife you all in your sleep? Unfortunately, I'm not as light-footed as I usually am, so I'm sure you'd hear my approach."

"I'm more concerned about what your brothers will do when they find out you're here."

So, this Adam wasn't a dummy. Martina had wondered the same. "They don't know I'm here. My brother Brock and his family are gone to New York City, and Tyler lives in Fort Worth. Besides, they're mostly civilized. I can't believe they would..." She broke off, recalling some recent heated conversations with her brothers. "Well, they don't know I'm here," she said, and walked through the door.

"And you're not worried that the evil Coltranes would do anything to hurt you?" Adam asked.

"Adam," Noah said in a stern voice.

She gave a short laugh. "As if Noah would let you," she said, then met Adam's gaze. "Besides, if Noah is any indication, all of you are into this honor thing in a big way. I'm willing to risk it." She turned back to Noah. "What can I bring you to drink?"

"I'm not thirsty."

She looked Noah in the eye. Heavens, he was going to be more difficult than a two-year-old. "I didn't ask if you were thirsty. I'm sure you remember the doctor said you needed to drink a lot of fluids. Would you like me to choose for you?"

Noah gave a slight groan. "Whiskey," he muttered under his breath. "Lemonade. Okay, bring me lemonade. Kitchen's straight ahead and to the left."

Noah watched her leave and took a moment to relish the sight of Martina in his home. Her dark hair bounced against her shoulders and her long, coltish legs made short work of the hall to the kitchen. From behind, he could barely tell she was pregnant. Her back was straight, her buttocks tight and round, and her legs still as sexy as the day he'd first met her.

"C'mon, I need to get you into bed. You have lost your mind," Adam said, shaking his head and acting as a crutch on the stairs. "Bringing Martina Logan into our house. Are you sure that concussion hasn't impaired your judgment?"

"My judgment's fine. It's these damn ribs and my gimpy leg." Accustomed to nearly unlimited energy, he despised his current weariness. "I feel like a toddler who needs a nap. I've been trying to get Martina out here since I found out she was pregnant.

When she volunteered, did you really think I was going to refuse her?''

"Only if you were thinking straight,'' Adam said.

"Absolutely not. Martina Logan has just fallen into my lap, and I may not be in the best condition, but I plan to take full advantage of the situation. If I have anything to say about it, she won't be leaving.''

Adam helped Noah around the corner to the bedroom. He rubbed his face with his hand and looked at Noah with an expression that mixed admiration and pity. "If she's gonna stay, you'd better get that house finished. The boys won't know what to do with a pregnant woman in the house. A Logan at that.''

Martina spent the day bringing Noah beverages, encouraging him to stay away from the computer, intercepting telephone calls and telling him to rest. Before today, she'd had no concept of how busy his plans for the ranch and trading on the stock market kept him. Keeping him from the computer and the phone presented an ongoing tug-of-war. By afternoon, she was tempted to spike his drink with a sleeping pill.

She glanced at the clock—11 p.m.—and gazed again at Noah. He was the most driven man she'd ever met in her life. All that passion drew and excited her at the same time that it repelled her. The thought struck her that he was so hard-driven, so much harder on himself than anyone else, that he could use a soft woman in his life.

In that case, Martina wryly thought, he didn't need her. She couldn't help but notice that the Coltrane home needed a woman's touch the way a flower needed rain, but adding a woman's touch to a bunch of rogue brothers in West Texas had never been her life's aspiration. Martina had always prized independence, respect and autonomy. In secret moments in the dark, she had wished for a special love with a man, but she'd never been able to meld her need for independence with her longing for love.

Looking at Noah with his mussed dark hair, black eyelashes against his tanned skin, and broad shoulders, she was struck anew by how complex he was. He was so strong it was difficult for her to imagine him needing anyone, especially her.

She lifted her hand to touch his forehead, then thought better of it and lowered her hand to her lap.

His eyes flickered open, and for a moment she wondered if he'd read her thoughts.

"You're supposed to be asleep," she whispered.

He glanced at the clock. "So are you."

"What do you want to drink with your pain medication?"

"No…" he began, and his lips twitched. "Just water."

Martina filled his glass in the bathroom that adjoined his bedroom to hers and brought it to him. He grimaced as he turned, but quickly downed the pills and water. "Thanks. Did you get anything to eat?"

"Yes, your brothers kept bringing me sandwiches. It was almost as if they thought I was a hungry animal and I'd get nasty if I didn't get fed."

His lips twitched again. "Can't imagine where they got that impression."

Realization hit Martina. "What did you tell them about me?"

"Just that feeding you tends to keep you in a good mood. You gotta remember we haven't had a woman around for a long time, so they don't really know what to do with you."

"You didn't seem to have that problem." The comment heedlessly popped out of her mouth.

His eyes darkened with sensual awareness. "I always thought it was important to learn what gives a woman pleasure."

"That sounds like you've had quite a bit of practice," she said.

"I've had a few relationships," he conceded. "No woman got me anywhere near the altar. Except you."

Martina opened her mouth to remind him of the very obvious point that the reason he wanted to get married wasn't that she had bowled him over. It was that she was pregnant with his child. He still had circles under his eyes and she could tell his ribs were hurting, so she didn't want to argue with him. He needed to sleep.

"I wasn't your first, either, Martina," Noah said quietly.

She closed her eyes, torn between revealing the truth and keeping her mouth shut.

"You didn't love me like a virgin would."

His assumption irritated her. She opened her eyes and looked at him. "How many virgins have you been with?"

He paused, rubbed his chin, then narrowed his eyes. "None."

"Then I guess you wouldn't know, would you?"

He looked at her in disbelief. "I can't believe you made it into your twenties without having a lover."

"Well, you might be forgetting my two older brothers, who pretty much threatened to cut off the genitals of any man who dated me longer than a month. I graduated from a women's college and I like my independence."

"But you made love to me like a woman who knows how to please a man."

"I didn't want you to know how inexperienced I was."

"Why me, then? Why me for your first lover? A man your family would hate. A man you couldn't share a future with."

"I think knowing I couldn't share a future with you was part of it. It made you safe. You wouldn't want to marry me any more than I would want to marry you."

He pinched the bridge of his nose as if his head

was aching. Concerned, Martina touched his shoulder. "Do you need some headache medication?"

"No, I just want to make sure I understand this. The entire reason you got involved with me was that you knew we wouldn't get married?"

Martina pulled away. "Well, no. That wasn't all of it. I was very attracted to you. I was probably even fascinated," she grudgingly revealed. "I loved the way your mind worked."

He glanced at her with a predatory glint in his eye and tugged her down onto his bed. "Still very attracted?"

Martina's heart stuttered. "You need to go to sleep."

He skimmed his finger down her bare arm. "You didn't answer my question. Still very attracted?"

She felt a shiver. "You really do need to rest."

He leaned forward, his lips a breath away from hers. "If you love the way my mind works, why do you fight me so much?"

Martina's mouth went dry and she tried to swallow. "You're a little overwhelming."

"Not for you," he said, rubbing his mouth against hers, creating a delicious buzz. "You're strong, sweetheart. You can take me anytime you want, so why don't you?"

Martina's stomach tightened. His mouth played over hers, teasing, taunting and inviting. He lifted her hand to his shoulder, as if offering his smooth skin and hard muscle for her pleasure.

He made it so easy to touch him and to want him
unbearably. He made it so easy to believe at this
moment that he would not deliberately bend her will
to his.

He slid his hands to the underside of her breasts
and gave a sigh that mixed desire and frustration.
"I want to make love to you."

A dozen yes and no replies stuck in her throat.
She swallowed hard. "You're still recovering. Your
ribs are broken, your lung—"

"You could have a healing effect on me," he
murmured, his thumbs moving closer to the tips of
her breasts.

Martina shook away the thick cloud of wanting.
"That's a ridiculous line," she whispered.

"Maybe we should stop talking."

His thumb glanced over her nipple and Martina
felt herself begin to melt. She fought it. "Maybe we
should start thinking," she said, and forced herself
to push away from him.

Standing, she resisted the urge to fan herself. She
felt hot from the inside out, and she knew the air
conditioner was running full blast. Filled to the brim
with such wanting, she feared she would turn into a
pillar of salt if she dared even to look at him.

"I've dreamed of making love to you in my bed."

Martina looked at his big bed with the golden oak
headboard and royal-blue coverlet. It was easy to
visualize him naked and wrapped around her. She
squished her eyes closed and banished the images

from her mind. "Go to sleep, Noah. You need your rest."

And Martina needed her sanity.

By the following Friday, Noah wanted to fight. Cooped up in the house with his ribs hurting, sitting up in bed every night, blowing into that damn lung machine every hour and having Martina in his house but not in his bed and not to stay made him want to kick down a few doors. To make matters worse, he couldn't even engage his brother Gideon in a good frustration-reducing fencing match because he wasn't supposed to raise his arms.

Martina appeared at his bedroom door with lemonade and more painkillers. He shook his head. The painkillers might fool him into thinking his ribs didn't hurt, but the inactivity they induced wasn't worth it.

"I'm not taking any more," he said, rising from the bed.

Martina gaped at him. "But—"

"But nothing. I'm not taking any more of those pills during the day." He bent down to pull on his boots and bit back a grimace.

"Wait a minute," she said. "I can help you—"

"I can put on my own boots," he told her.

"Cabin fever?" she asked with far more sympathy than he deserved at the moment.

He scowled, brushed past her and stomped down the stairs. Squinting his eyes against the late-afternoon sun, he headed for the horse barn. He'd almost broken a sweat by the time he reached it, and he swore under his breath at how his body wasn't performing. Accustomed to pushing himself physically and mentally, he had little patience for sluggishness.

He broke the doctor's rule about lifting his arms and saddled his black horse, Thunder. Riding, he knew, would clear his muddy head. He guided the horse out of the barn and mounted him, liking the feel of his feet in the stirrups and the leather reins in his hands. Something inside him eased at the familiar sensation of horseflesh beneath him, and he took off in a trot that quickly turned into a gallop.

He was still sore from the automobile accident, and it occurred to him that he could have used a few spark plugs for this ride. But the wind in his face erased the comatose feeling he'd been fighting.

Riding toward the south pasture, he slowed when he caught sight of cattle. He rode a little farther until he saw the stream that joined Coltrane property with Logan property. The water represented one of the ongoing sources of conflict between Noah's family and Martina's. Their child, he feared, could be the greatest source of conflict the two families had ever experienced.

Not if he could stop it, he thought, determination coursing through him. He swung off his horse and looped the reins over a tree, then strolled toward the stream. He gazed at the Logan land on the other side. The grass had always looked greener, the cows fatter, and everything in general had appeared easier for the Logans.

He thought about Martina and what a powerful mix of woman she was, strong, beautiful, vulnerable. She didn't know the impact she'd had on him from the moment he'd looked into her eyes. He wouldn't call it love, because he'd long ago decided a man shouldn't place his bets on romantic love. His passion had been improving his family's situation.

Although he wouldn't deny his passion for Martina, he didn't want his emotions to get in the way of persuading her to marry him. It was right for them to be together. He knew it in his gut and in his bones. He knew he wanted her more than he should. The idea of losing her made him break into a cold sweat. She was the woman who carried his child, the woman who filled his mind with dreams and tested his mind's ability to rule his heart.

Remembering how his life had been without her, he felt his gut clench and he scowled. She was too important for him to let his emotions get out of control. She kept him on his toes, yet made everything inside him click. Later, after they had married, maybe he would be able to trust her enough to let go a little. But not now, he thought. Too much was at stake.

Martina glanced past her laptop computer screen out the window, searching for Noah. She shouldn't care. She certainly shouldn't worry. "He's a grown man," she muttered. "He can take care of himself."

"He'll come home twice as sore as he was when he left, but three times happier," a male voice said from behind her.

Martina turned and saw Jonathan in her open doorway. The brothers had been scarce around her, almost as if they were afraid of her. Martina knew that couldn't be true. "This is one of those self-destructive patterns men sometimes exhibit?" she asked.

Jonathan nodded, remaining in the doorway. "Yeah, but it's also a survival thing. Get out or go crazy."

Martina slid her glance toward the window once more, then back to Jonathan. "You can come in. Despite the stories I'm sure you've been told, I don't bite."

"I don't think I heard anything about biting," Jonathan said in a noncommittal tone, his mouth twitching as he slowly entered the room. She noticed his slight limp again and wondered what had caused it.

"What did you hear?"

He shrugged. "I don't know. Something about a pregnant porcupine."

Martina chuckled. "Well, that would be true. This pregnancy has definitely brought out my quills."

"What are you going to do with my brother?"

Martina blinked at the directness of his gaze and

his question. It was the same kind of question she might have expected one of her own brothers to direct at Noah. "I'm not sure. I didn't plan to get pregnant, so I never planned anything permanent with Noah." A subconscious delusional dream perhaps, but she'd never planned.

"He's not a bad guy. Well educated, he's the only one of us to get a master's degree. Of course, everything he got, he got with scholarships. He's smart, honorable and he would protect you with his life."

Yes, but would he love me with all his heart? Martina's heart squeezed at the same time that she was touched by Jonathan's comments. "Are you his PR man?"

"He doesn't need one," Jonathan said. "Sometimes people get themselves in situations where they don't see straight."

"Are you suggesting that I can't see straight?"

"I'm suggesting that you're in a situation where it might be hard for you to see Noah clearly."

She took a careful breath. "I know he's a good man. He's probably a wonderful man, but your family and my family:..." She lifted her shoulders.

Jonathan nodded. "Yeah. Bad music between the Logans and Coltranes for a long time. Of course, us Coltranes have been fighting our bad rep since we were born. That black-sheep stuff gets old when all you want to do is ask a girl to dance, let alone try to court her. Gideon says we're all going to have to import brides like they did in the Old West," Jonathan said. "Gideon has a great imagination. We were able to send him to college, and he has a decent head for business, but we're beginning to think he majored in girls and frat parties."

"Why didn't you go to college?" Martina asked.

"I did the rodeo." He cocked his head to one side. "That's how I got the limp. Adam would give his eye teeth for a degree. He's always reading. We call him Abe Lincoln when he's not around."

This was the first extended conversation Martina had ever had with any of the Coltrane brothers, and she found herself hungry for more information. "Why doesn't Adam get his degree?"

"He can't leave the ranch. He's the cattle expert."

"But he doesn't have to leave. He could earn a degree on-line." Martina pointed to her computer.

Jonathan raised his eyebrows. "Is that so?" He walked closer to her. "We had this foreman who taught all of us how to fence," he said.

"Zachary," Martina said.

Surprise shot through his eyes. "Yeah. He kept us from ending up in jail, and he was always telling us that we should never stop learning."

"And how do you keep learning?"

He looked self-conscious. "I like music. I listen to classical stuff a lot."

"Do you play piano or...?"

"I never had lessons."

"Me, neither. My mother played and taught both my brothers, but she died when I was born, and my father didn't want anyone touching the piano after she was gone.'' Martina stopped, surprised at how easy it was to reveal something so personal to a stranger. A Coltrane, at that.

He looked at her with a hint of understanding in his eyes, then shook his head. "We always thought the Logans had it perfect, but I guess everybody has their problems.'' He glanced beyond her out the window. "Here he comes. He's gonna feel like a piece of tobacco that's been chewed and spit out.''

Martina looked out the window, spotting Noah walk, with a slight limp, toward the house.

"He's a good man, Martina. You could do worse for your baby.''

Her heart tightened. "I know, but there's more to it than the fact that he's a good man.''

"The Coltranes and Logans have been making bad music for a long time. Maybe it's time to change the tune.''

Martina remained silent and torn. Even if they could put all the bad blood between their families in the past, Martina wasn't sure she could spend the rest of her life trying to make another man love her.

Nine

"I need you to stay," Noah said the following night just as Martina started to leave his bedroom.

She turned back to face him, wishing for the hundredth time that he would wear a shirt so her gaze wouldn't wander to his broad shoulders and muscular chest. She was never unaware of the physical power of his masculinity. She was beginning to feel as if she was fighting a landslide by fighting her involvement with Noah. How could she remain close to him and continue to tell herself she didn't want him, mind, body and heart?

Keeping her gaze above his throat didn't help, she thought. His eyes did things to her. They always had. "Why?" she asked, trying to keep the edginess from her voice.

A wave of self-consciousness flashed across his face. It was so rare an expression for him she almost didn't catch it.

"I need to read," he said.

Puzzled, she frowned. "Is this a late aftereffect of your concussion? Do you need me to read to you?"

"No. I need to read," he said, shoving his hands in his jean pockets, "and you need to be in the room. Close by."

Still confused, she walked closer. "Okay. Where should I sit?"

"The bed's fine," he said.

Martina glanced at him sideways.

"This isn't a seduction," he said. "It sounds a little hokey, but Adam read this article about how reading to babies while they're in the womb increases their intelligence."

Amused, but mostly touched, Martina sat on his bed. "You want to read to the baby."

He shrugged and nodded. "Yeah."

Her heart contracted. "Okay. What did you have in mind? Not stock reports."

He chuckled darkly. "No. Adam suggested *War and Peace,* but I told him that might be kinda heavy for a baby."

"So what did you choose?"

He picked up a book from the nightstand. "*The

Hobbit,'' he said. ''I figure between the two of us this child will get plenty of adventure genes, so we might as well let her get started.''

And so Noah sat next to her on his big bed and began to read the wondrous story of how boring, respectable and comfortable Bilbo Baggins got suckered into a wild and dangerous adventure.

And with each passing word of his baritone voice, Martina fell for him a little more. Noah had lied when he'd said this wasn't a seduction. It was a seduction of the most secret places in her heart. Although she'd occasionally badgered her brothers into reading to her when she was a child, her father had never read to her. She would have given up ice cream for a year just to have her father read the sports section of the newspaper to her.

When Noah finished the first chapter, he put the book back on the nightstand and gazed at her in an assessing way. ''You're very quiet.''

''I was listening.'' *And feeling too much. Wanting too much.*

''You're thinking I'm crazy.''

No, I'm thinking I am crazy. ''Not at all,'' she said. ''Did your father read to you?''

''Never,'' Noah said. ''I will be a better father than my father was.''

She watched him rub the back of his neck and could tell he was tired. ''Why don't you get ready for bed and let me rub your neck for you?''

Surprise chased near refusal chased quiet curiosity

across his face. "Okay," he finally said. "Give me a couple of minutes."

He washed up in the bathroom and returned wearing briefs and nothing else. Martina suspected he'd kept on the briefs in deference to her, but they hid little. The air grew thick as she breathed. "I'll sit behind you since you can't lie down," she offered, and moved farther back on the bed to make room for him.

He sat down and she tentatively lifted her fingers to his corded neck. She kneaded the tight muscles and massaged his shoulders. His tension showed in the knots she rubbed.

Noah made a rough sound of appreciation. "I don't remember you being such a good masseuse."

"We didn't have a lot of time," she said, "for taking time."

He caught her hand and brought it to his lips. "That was wrong."

Her heart tripped over itself. "You're tired. You should go to sleep."

"You should stay with me tonight," he murmured.

"Maybe I will." The words popped out of her mouth, but originated in her heart.

She felt him stop breathing. He turned carefully and eased back against the pillows propped in front of the headboard. He chuckled and covered a wide yawn. "You would pick a night when I can barely keep my eyes open."

Martina smiled to cover her nerves. "I'm ornery that way."

He held out his arm. "Then be ornery next to me."

She moved to his side and reached to turn out the light. A suspended awareness seemed to swell in the very air around her. In the darkness, she lightly pressed her cheek to Noah's chest and felt the beating of his heart. She pulled back slightly and he stopped her by curling his hand over her cheek.

"Stay," he muttered.

"I can't lean on your ribs. I might hurt you." She entwined her fingers through his and slowly lowered her cheek to a pillow. "Go to sleep," she whispered.

Too tense, too aware of him to relax, Martina lay stiffly beside him absorbing the rhythm of his breaths and the sensation of his strong hand in hers. A score of emotions tugged at her—anxiety, tenderness, desire, uneasiness. But through them all, she had the odd sense that she was where she was supposed to be. Her mind and her brothers and the rest of the world could argue with her until sunrise, but Martina felt she was where she belonged.

If only until sunrise.

Hours later, she awakened to the sensation of Noah's hands on her bare belly. "What?"

"It's okay," he said, his voice both sensual and reassuring. "It's just me."

Just me, Martina thought. When had Noah ever been *just anything?*

"I keep having this dream where I'm touching your belly and the baby is moving." He brushed his finger over her lips. "And you're kissing me."

Martina licked her lips, her tongue glancing over his finger. His eyes lit like twin fires, and he slid his finger into her mouth. The small sensual invasion kicked the doors off her denial of the past months. This man could make her want like no other. She suckled gently on his finger and he groaned, then urged her onto his lap.

Lifting her shirt, he splayed his hands over her bare belly and held her with his gaze. "Kiss me."

His words were a combination order and plea she couldn't refuse. Martina slowly leaned forward and rubbed her mouth against his. He darted his tongue over her lips and inside, tasting her, taking her. His warmth and passion moved over her like a wave of heat on a hot Texas afternoon. Her heart pounded against her rib cage and her body temperature soared. She touched his chest and felt his heart pound against her palm. Could he really want her so much?

Noah pulled her shirt upward, stopping at her neck as if he was loath to pull his mouth from hers. With a reluctant sigh, he pulled away slightly and tugged the shirt over her head. He gazed at her bare torso and pushed her panties low on her belly. "Oh, Martina, you have no idea what seeing you like this does to me." He shifted and lifted his dark, frankly sexual gaze to hers. "But you will. Up on your knees darlin'," he told her.

Martina complied. "Why?"

"Closer," he said, wrapping his large hands around her bottom and bringing her belly directly in front of his face.

Then he ran his hands all over her abdomen and followed with his mouth. His mouth on her ripe midsection was the most erotic sight of her life. She felt herself turn to liquid in all her secret places.

As he rubbed his cheek against her stomach, he lifted his hands and unfastened her bra. He ran his hands lightly over her breasts, finding her nipples already hard. "I would never have thought I could have wanted you more than I did in Chicago, but I was wrong," he said, and drew her lower so he could take her breast into his mouth.

Dispensing with her panties, he slid his fingers between her thighs and gently stroked her. Martina had never felt so voluptuously desirable. He made her ache for his possession. Each stroke of his tongue over her nipple and each flick of his finger over her femininity drove her closer to a frenzy of need. She tried, unsuccessfully, to bite back a moan.

Noah pulled back, his eyes nearly black with sexual intent. "What do you want?"

She shuddered as he continued to stroke her. "You in me. I want you in me."

He swore. "I don't want to hurt you."

She shook her head. "You won't."

"Are you sure?"

She nodded, swollen with wanting.

He quickly ditched his briefs and drew her hand to his full erection. He kissed her mouth as she stroked him. Touching wasn't enough, so she pulled back and lowered her mouth to kiss him intimately.

Noah let out a low groan. His thighs taut as bands against her breasts, he allowed her to take him into her mouth, but only for a moment. "I can't last, baby. Come to me."

On trembling knees, she mounted him, and at his deliciously full invasion, her moan mingled with his. For one powerful moment, they gazed into each other's eyes, joined at last. The evidence of their previous passion for each other, her ripe belly, served as yet another erotic, emotional reminder of their bond. Filled with Noah in the most basic way, she felt her landslide of emotions tumbling her more deeply toward him.

It was more than want, more than need, something terribly close to love. Closing her eyes against a shot of fear, she undulated slightly and heard his groan of pleasure.

"Come here," he said, and drew her mouth to his as he cupped his hands around her bottom and led her in a mind-bending rhythm. Everything but Noah faded from her existence.

Lifting one hand, he stroked her jaw as he consumed her with his mouth and tongue, echoing their deeper intimacy. Swollen with anticipation, Martina felt her body tighten around his shaft. The combination was too much. She shattered around him, her climax shuddering through her in fits and starts.

Noah gave a low groan that vibrated through her mouth, through her very being, as he spilled his pleasure into her. Martina felt her bond with him in every pore of her body.

The first sliver of dawn's pale light woke her the next morning. She blinked her eyes and was immediately aware of Noah. Her cheek rested against his arm, her belly against his side. She was naked and so was he. Although he was propped against the pillows, she could still see the peaceful rise and fall of his chest.

For a moment she wondered what it would be like to wake up in his bed and arms every morning. The forbidden image of looking into his eyes at the start of every day taunted her.

What about their families? And what if he only wanted her and never grew to love her? Her stomach tightened with fear. The baby moved inside her and she felt so torn that tears sprang to her eyes.

She had to get away from Noah, Martina thought. She needed to clear her head, and with him so close she didn't stand a chance. Not bothering with her clothes, she eased out of the covers and carefully slid out of bed, then tiptoed to the bathroom that connected Noah's room with hers. She closed the door, locked it and breathed.

Although he had been gentle, her nipples were tender and a few pink marks colored her skin. She had been completely enveloped by him, and she struggled with a sense of being overwhelmed. Much was at stake.

Biting her lip, she turned on the shower jets and stepped inside the bathtub. *A clear head,* she told herself. *I need a clear head.*

As the commodities exchange would have it, Martina successfully avoided Noah throughout the morning. She had left early to go to the grocery store, and when she returned been told that he had asked for her. Since then, he'd been engrossed in taking advantage of a volatile day on the market.

Martina was no less confused. Making love with Noah had solved nothing. They still had the same problems. The only thing making love with him had shown her was the power of their passion for each other and the incredible bond they shared.

But how long would that bond remain if they didn't truly love each other? Martina feared she was fooling herself with that question. It was frightening to admit to herself, but she loved Noah Coltrane. She could hide it from everyone else, but she couldn't dodge it herself any longer.

She was wise enough to know that one-sided love didn't work. How long would their bond remain if Noah never loved her?

Pensive, she paced the downstairs living room. She didn't know which was the most blah room in the house, but this one came close. Beige walls, beige sofa, brown chair. The house desperately needed some color. It desperately needed a woman, but not her, Martina thought. She was far too independent and opinionated for the Coltrane brotherhood. She would drive them all straight up the wall.

The phone rang. Martina knew Patch, the cook, was out in the garden and everyone except Noah was outside. She hesitated to answer on the off chance that one of her brothers might guess her whereabouts. It continued to ring, and since she knew Noah was glued to the monitor and refused to talk on the phone when he was trading, she picked up. "Hello?"

There was a silent pause. "Is this the Coltrane residence?" a female voice asked.

"Yes, it is," Martina replied, her curiosity growing.

"I'd like to speak to Noah Coltrane, please."

Martina felt a sinking sensation in her stomach. "He can't come to the phone right now. Can I take a message?"

"This is Wendy Holden, and Noah and I had dinner a few months ago in Dallas. I own a travel agency and I'd like to discuss his fencing camp. Tell him to give me a call, and this time, I'll give him a home-cooked meal in my home. That way we can avoid interruptions," she said in a smoky voice.

Martina felt the ugly scrape of jealousy. Fierce, intense possessiveness coursed through her. She took a careful breath. "I'll give him the message. Does he have your number?"

Wendy, whom Martina was certain was blond, thin and had no problems with swelling ankles, happily recited her number and hung up. *Wendy* probably had no problem seeing her toes.

Martina nearly broke the pencil lead as she wrote the message for Noah. She was so upset she could pop. When had he seen her? Who else had he courted and seduced during the time they'd been apart?

While she'd been heaving with morning sickness, he could well have been seducing half of Texas. Make that Texas and Chicago.

Martina knew she wasn't being rational, but the inviting tone in the woman's voice pushed all the wrong buttons. She stared at the beige wall and decided she couldn't stay in this house one minute longer. She heard the back door slam, signaling Patch's return.

She made tracks to the kitchen and placed the offending message on the kitchen table. "I need to go out for a while. Please make sure Noah gets this message."

"Where you going?" the small, older man called after her.

"Out," Martina replied as she stepped through the front doorway and headed for her car. She needed to think.

As he watched his last trade of the day fill, Noah finally took a breath. The market had been especially volatile today, and since he'd been out of commission several days this week, he'd wanted to take advantage of his opportunities. He felt stiff and sore, and he wanted to see Martina.

She had made love with him with such abandon last night. It had been better, more powerful than he remembered. She had the strange ability to satisfy him completely at the same time that she made him want more.

He stood and resisted the urge to stretch, knowing it would hurt more than it would help. He could tell his lung was better. He didn't feel the damn rattle every time he breathed. Sick of babying his ribs, he figured he'd still have to put up with sleeping upright a while longer.

Noah couldn't deny he was improving, but he was determined to find a way to keep Martina with him. Last night was a start. He wondered where she was. "Martina," he called, whipping open his door. "Martina."

"She's not here," Patch said, appearing at the bottom of the steps and waving a piece of paper. "She told me to make sure you got this message, then she left."

Noah frowned as he made his way down the stairs. "Left? Where'd she go?"

Patch shrugged. "When I asked her, she said,

'Out.'" He raised his bushy gray eyebrows. "You might want to read the message."

Noah scanned the piece of paper and felt his gut sink. Wendy Holden was a man-eater and proud of it. His only interest in her had been her suggestion to promote the ranch's fencing and roundup weekends through her travel agency. When Wendy had indicated she wanted more, Noah had sought other avenues for promoting the ranch's expansion activities. Martina didn't know any of that, though. He could easily imagine what had gone through that pretty head of hers. "Damn," he muttered. "She didn't say anything about where she was going?"

"Out," Patch repeated with emphasis. "That was the last word I heard before the door slammed behind her. She took her car."

"Damn," Noah said again, and took the steps two at a time. If she was leaving permanently, she might have left her clothes, but would have taken her computer, he thought, swinging open her bedroom door to view her room. Her laptop was still on the small desk. He gave a small sigh of relief.

He stood in her room and stroked his chin, thinking. *If I were Martina and I was upset as hell, where would I go?*

An answer immediately came to him. An answer that did not please him. His gut twisted. "Damn," he said for the third time, and headed for his brother Adam's truck.

Ten

Noah spotted Martina's blue Mustang just as the Logan house came into view. He felt an odd mix of relief and ingrained wariness as he looked at the large, impressive home. Damn. Sometimes he hated being right.

The pretty house, the pretty flowers and the pretty life represented the exact opposite of what the Coltrane ranch had to offer. He narrowed his eyes as he pulled the truck to a stop. That was in the past. If they wanted, the Coltranes could plant flowers with the best of them.

He swung out of the truck and headed for the front door, stiffening his spine in preparation for battle with Martina's family. He punched the bell and glared at the door as he waited.

The housekeeper answered the door, casting a suspicious look at him. "Good afternoon, Mr. Logan."

"I need to see Martina," he told the woman.

"She's in the library. I'll have to ask if she's receiving visitors," the housekeeper said with a sniff.

Noah made a face at the woman's back and didn't wait for an invitation. "I'll announce myself," he said, brushing past her.

"If she shoots you with one of her daddy's rifles, don't say I didn't warn you. She ain't in a pretty mood."

He paused at the wry tone in the housekeeper's voice and offered his own wry grin as he tipped his hat. "Thank you very much, Miss..."

"Addie," she said with a look of pleased surprise at his politeness. "The library's at the end of the hall. Good luck."

He took in the comfort and beauty of Martina's childhood home and felt his gut tighten. A woman could feel at home here, whereas at the Coltrane ranch... He stopped just outside the last open doorway.

Martina stood, shredding the stuffings of a pillow. Small wads of the stuff clumped around her feet. She made a whimpering sound that clutched at his heart. "I wish you were here," she said. "A million times I've wished it, but never more than now."

She must have sensed his presence because she looked up and saw him in the doorway. She shredded another piece of stuffing. "Go away."

"Like hell I will," he said, walking into the room. "What do you think you're doing taking off and not telling anyone where you're going? You're pregnant. You can't do that."

"Addie would have helped me handle any emergency. She still will." Martina frowned. "I can't believe she let you in," she said, shooting him a look of disdain.

"If this is about Wendy..." he began.

"Ah, yes." She smiled sweetly. Too sweetly. "Wendy, Wendy, Wendy. She sounded like she very much enjoyed the dinner you two shared a few months ago—"

"Nothing happened," he interjected.

"—while I was spending every morning hugging the porcelain bowl," she continued as if he hadn't spoken, "and you were apparently sowing your seed all over Texas."

Noah narrowed his eyes and moved closer, crowding her. "You just hold on to that knife you call a tongue. The only thing I was sowing with Wendy was the possibility that her travel agency might promote my fencing camps and roundup weekends. You may have forgotten the fact that I just learned I was fathering a child a month ago, but I haven't. You haven't given a tinker's damn what I've been doing by myself, let alone with another woman, for the last seven months, so why do you care now?''

He held her laser-sharp blue gaze. ''You walked out on me with no warning. If you expect me to live like a monk just because you made love with me, then left me like yesterday's garbage, then...'' He took a deep breath. ''Then you'd be right.''

She blinked, her eyes shiny with tears. ''Oh, I can't believe you lived like a monk.''

''Believe it.'' His heart swelled with such confusing emotions that he looked away to gather his wits. His gaze landed on a portrait of a woman who looked exactly like Martina. ''Is it you? Is that—''

''My mother,'' she said, sniffing. ''I'm told I look a lot like her.''

Blinking, he stared at the picture and shook his head. ''The resemblance is incredible.'' When he realized she had been talking to the portrait when he'd first seen her, his chest grew tight.

Martina hugged the shredded pillow to her chest. ''That's what everyone says. That's why he couldn't stand to look at me,'' she said, nodding toward the portrait beside her mother's.

Martina's father. He had been a hard man, Noah concluded from the picture and what he'd heard of the man's reputation. Losing his wife hadn't softened him.

Noah gazed at Martina and saw the look of an orphan in her blue eyes. He put an arm around her shoulders. ''Why'd you come here?''

"I needed to go somewhere that I belonged," she said.

Noah gritted his teeth at the surprising stab of pain her words caused. "Haven't you learned you belong with me?"

She drew in a deep breath and sighed. "I'm not sure about that."

Impatience tore at him. "What's not to be sure? I'm the father of your child. I will be good to you and the baby. You can count on that."

She stepped away from him. "I want more than that."

"What do you mean?"

"I mean, I spent my whole childhood trying to get my father to love me. I don't want to spend my whole adult life trying to get a husband to love me."

Noah felt caught between a rock and a hard place. "You mean a lot to me," he said, but the words sounded insubstantial to his own ears. He tried again. "I want you more than any woman. You know I care about you."

"But you don't love me."

He shoved his hands in his pockets. "I've always thought love was unpredictable at best, not something a man with any sense bets much of his gold on. Other things like family and commitment are more important." He could tell he wasn't getting through to her. Frustration raked across him. "There are some things too important to let emotions mess up. You are one of them."

Her eyebrows furrowed in confusion and indecision. Although Noah firmly believed in allowing each individual his or her freedom to choose, at this moment, he wished he could choose for Martina.

"You don't believe in love?"

"I didn't say that," he asserted. "I just don't bank on it. Here's an example. What if I had decided I'd fallen in love with you when we met in Chicago? After you left me, what was I supposed to think?"

Quiet for a long thoughtful moment, she seemed to have stepped outside herself. "Did it hurt you when I left?"

Noah immediately felt a barrier go up inside him. He looked away and struggled to answer her question honestly. "Yeah," he finally said. "It did. And it hurt even more to find out you were pregnant and hadn't gotten around to telling me."

"How much did it hurt?" Martina asked, shredding the stuffing of the pillow again.

He remembered the pain that had dulled only when he'd lost himself in his work. At night, however, he'd been unable to escape it. "I couldn't sleep," he reluctantly revealed.

She bit her lip. "This is a mess," she said in a broken voice.

"Yeah, you've mutilated that pillow."

Martina glanced down at the pillow and made a sound somewhere between a sob and a chuckle. "I wasn't talking about the pillow. I was talking about us and our situation. I don't see how it can work."

The hopelessness in her eyes cut like one of his swords. "Let me take care of it. I'm known for my innovative solutions."

"This is going to take a miracle."

"I've never let that stop me before. What are you afraid of, Martina?"

"That I'll never know what it feels like to have a husband who loves me. That I'll disappoint my brothers if I stay with you. That the Logan curse will cause a lot of heartbreak."

"You don't really believe in that curse, do you?"

"It's hard not to believe when I heard about it all the time from my father. There's a lot at stake here, Noah."

"I know, Martina. You can count on me."

Doubt shimmered in her eyes. He longed for her unswerving confidence, but understood he had yet to earn it. He had time, he told himself. Not as much as he'd like, but he had time.

She walked toward the baby grand in the center of the room. "My mother played this piano. She taught my brothers, but I never learned."

"You're still carrying on her tradition," he told her.

"How?" she asked skeptically. "I can't even play 'Chopsticks.'"

"You play a different kind of keys," he said. "Computer keys."

A slow smile lifted her lips and subsequently his

heart at the same time. "I never thought of it that way."

He crossed to her and pulled her into his arms. "Come home with me. You want to hear chapter two of *The Hobbit*."

She looked torn. "I can't stay with you much longer," she said. "My brother Brock and his family will return from New York, and I don't like concealing my whereabouts from him or Tyler. I owe them that much."

"What do you owe them, Martina?" he asked. "Now that you're a grown woman ready to give birth to our first child, what do you owe your brothers?"

She bit her lip and shredded more pillow stuffing. "I don't know, but I do know I hate feeling disloyal to them." She shook her head as if she wanted to shake off the discussion. "Addie has homegrown tomatoes for me. And I crave homegrown tomatoes so much I would probably trade my body for them."

Noah tucked that vivid image-inducing comment in the back of his mind and took the pitiful-looking pillow from her arms. "Is surgery possible, or should we go ahead and dig the grave?"

"We can always send it to Wendy," she said in that too-sweet voice again as she turned and walked from the room.

Watching her, Noah wasn't offended by the dig. If Martina was the tiniest bit possessive, then perhaps she could be possessed.

Martina listened to the second chapter of *The Hobbit* and fought the lulling seductiveness of Noah's voice. She remembered the way he'd touched her the night before. She remembered how right it had felt, so right to be possessed by him, to possess him. But she was fooling herself because although she might have a piece of Noah's heart, she would never have all of it. Would that be enough to last her the rest of her life?

Her stomach twisted and desperation tightened the back of her throat. The whole situation felt like a no-win for everyone involved, even the baby. That thought tore at her.

She needed to go back to her condo in Dallas. She needed to think clearly. This was too important. Noah was right about that. In the meantime, she wished Noah would stop going shirtless and get laryngitis.

Her heart and body softened just hearing him read. Which showed how insane he was making her. She bit back a sigh of disgust at her reaction to him. Looking at him in the glow of the lamplight, she knew he would make it so easy to fall into his arms and bed, but she'd learned making love with him would just confuse her further.

As he finished the last words of the second chapter and closed the book, Martina sprang from the bed. "Well, I'm beat and I'm sure you are, too. Good ni—"

Noah stood and took her hand. "No need to rush," he said, pulling her to him.

Oh, yes, there is, she thought. "I need to go to bed," she said, trying very hard to ignore the way her heart raced and the fact that he stood before her nearly naked. "Without you."

He toyed with her hair. "Why?"

"Because making love with you isn't a good idea," she said.

"You didn't like it?"

His gaze wrapped around her with a combination of warmth and seduction. "I didn't say that. You told me that you didn't want emotions getting in the way of your thinking, that this situation is too important. I think you're right, so we shouldn't make love."

"How do you know that making love with me doesn't make you see everything more clearly?"

Because my brain turns to mush when you are within five feet of me. His fingers in her hair had a drugging effect on her. It was all she could do not to lean into him and put her hands on his bare shoulders. She could easily drown in his eyes.

"I just know," she said. "So I'll go."

"Just one moment," he said, and eased his hand under her shirt to her bare belly at the same time that he lowered his mouth to hers. "I want to say good-night to both of you," he murmured, and kissed her and caressed her abdomen.

Martina willed herself not to melt, but his hands

were both soothing and arousing, his mouth both
gentle and seductive. His clean, musky smell and
the promise of all the sensation and emotion he
stirred in her drew her. Noah made her feel everything in 3-D Technicolor. She could have kissed him
and let him touch her all night.

And if she didn't move away, she was going to
dissolve into a puddle on this very spot.

Her heart and body protesting, she moved backward unsteadily. Noah's arms shot out to stabilize
her, sending her emotions into another tailspin. She
lifted her hands and took another step backward.
G'night, Noah.

When Martina awoke the next morning, she
opened her eyes to a bowl of fully ripe homegrown
tomatoes on her dresser. On them perched a note in
Noah's bold handwriting. "Tomatoes for you every
morning. You with me every evening. Fair trade?
Yours, Noah."

Martina didn't know whether to laugh or cry. She
had no intention of telling Noah he left homegrown
tomatoes in the dust even if it *was* an absolute fact.
If he wasn't so nearly perfect, she'd kick him. She
had to leave soon or she would give in to him.

That evening, Noah was edgy as hell. He was
getting better and he couldn't fake it, and Martina
was going to leave. He could feel it in his bones.
Why couldn't he get through to her?

After dinner, he reviewed some stock charts, then

returned downstairs. He heard Martina and Jonathan laughing in the living room. The sound drew him. He walked closer and heard her voice.

"One, two, three. One, two, three," she said. "See? You can do it. Who told you that you can't dance?"

"My leg isn't helping much, but it's not as bad as it would be if it were raining. This is the waltz? Damn, I never thought I'd see the day I'd be waltzing."

"With a very pregnant lady, no less," she said with another chuckle that made Noah's nerve endings crinkle.

"We're some kind of pair. The limping horse whisperer and…"

"The pregnant porcupine?" she suggested.

"I wasn't gonna say that."

"No." Martina's voice bubbled with amusement. "You were just thinking it."

Noah felt his gut twist with an emotion he couldn't immediately name. If Martina was going to *pair* with anyone, it was going to be him. Jealousy? Shock raced through him. He was jealous of his brother? He must be losing his mind, he thought, but the feeling didn't fade as he heard their continuing banter. Why was it so easy for Martina and Jonathan? Why did she smile and laugh with Jonathan when she avoided Noah as if he were the evil dragon from *The Hobbit?* Why? he wondered as he listened.

"Let me know if you get tired," Jonathan said. "Are you sure pregnant women are supposed to dance?"

"Pregnant women can do anything their doctors tell them they can do."

"You're sure about that?" Jonathan said.

"I'm sure. Are you afraid I'm going to have the baby in the middle of the living room just because I waltzed with you?"

Jonathan blanched and stopped midstep. "You wouldn't do that, would you?"

Martina shook her head and laughed. She had learned that Jonathan was the most easygoing of the Coltrane brothers. He provided a welcome break from all the tension she felt with the other brothers, including Noah. "I imagine it's going to take more than a waltz to pry this one out of me. You have to remember this baby has inherited stubbornness genes from both Noah and me."

"You and Noah are gonna have your hands full," Jonathan warned her.

"I didn't know dance lessons were on the schedule," Noah said, entering the room. "Where do I sign up?"

Martina stiffened and stepped on Jonathan's foot. He winced.

"Oh, I'm sorry. Maybe I'm not the best teacher."

"The best I ever had," he said.

From the corner of her eye, Martina saw Noah's frown deepen.

"The best you ever had," Noah echoed in a deceptively mild voice.

Jonathan did a double take. "Best *dance* teacher," he said to his brother, and slowly stepped away from Martina. "Thanks for the dance lesson." He shook his head at Noah. "I think I'll get a beer."

He left and an uneasy silence descended. "Would you like to go out on the porch?" Noah asked.

Confused and uneasy, Martina shrugged. "Okay."

She followed him outside, not standing too close. It was a warm, cloudless night, but the breeze made it more bearable. She drew in a deep breath and gazed up at the big Texas sky. "I like being able to order pizza and Chinese food and have them delivered in Dallas, but I sure do miss the stars. The city lights detract. Every now and then it's nice to look at a sky full of stars."

"Are you a city girl or country girl, Martina?"

"Both," she said. "I enjoy the conveniences of city life, but I need the quietness of the country at times."

Noah was in an odd mood. She could sense it, and it made her tense and uncomfortable.

After a long silence, Noah finally spoke again. "You and Jonathan seemed to get along well."

"He talks to me."

"What do you mean?" Noah asked, studying her.

"Your other brothers don't speak to me. I know they wish I wasn't here. Especially Adam. I can't say I blame them, but Jonathan doesn't mind talking to me, and he doesn't really expect anything of me.''

''I saw you laughing in his arms when I came downstairs,'' Noah said.

Realization and surprise raced through her. ''You can't think there's anything going on between Jonathan and me. Not if you have half a brain.''

He leaned against a railing. ''Maybe I don't where you're concerned,'' he muttered. ''He's just a man. He could fall for you.''

Martina stared at Noah in disbelief. ''Do you have a screw loose? Look at me,'' she said. ''Really look at me and tell me, what do you see?''

He looked at her for a long time. He looked at her so long Martina resisted the urge to squirm. ''I see a beautiful woman pregnant with my child,'' he said quietly.

Martina groaned. ''I appreciate the beautiful part. That's very nice, but the truth of the matter is, I have a lot in common with the *Titanic* at the moment. I am not *gently* pregnant. Most men who look at me are either filled with horrified curiosity or fear that I'm going to give birth any minute. I can tell you they are not looking at me with lust. And the only reason you might have any lust is because you are the fa—'' She cut herself off, not wanting to say the words, not wanting to reinforce the connection between them.

''Because I am the what, Martina? Finish what you were going to say.'' Noah moved closer to her.

Her heart jumped. "I…I was just going to say something about you donating genetic material."

"No, you weren't," he said, gently backing her against the wall. "You were going to say something else. Tell me, Martina."

"I…I…" She swallowed at the fierce expression on his face.

"What were you going to say?"

Trapped, she glared at him. "Okay, I was going to say you're the father. It doesn't change anything for me to say it. I'm still leaving tomorrow."

Eleven

"This cigar sucks," Noah said, tossing the stub of one of Gideon's cigars over the porch railing.

"I coulda told you that," Jonathan said, strolling onto the front porch. "Gideon could see you were miserable as hell and in his ignorance he thought a cigar would make you feel better."

Noah knew Jonathan and Gideon were holding an ongoing battle over Gideon's cigar usage. Ever since Jonathan had permanently hurt his leg in the rodeo, he'd become a different man, leading a cleaner life and taking more pleasure in simple things. More than ever, he was the peacemaker among Noah and his brothers. In fact his battle with Gideon was conducted with a more mild, verbal reproach, rather than stinging insults.

Noah longed for the easy, reassuring relationship he'd always shared with Jonathan, but at the moment, he wasn't sure if his brother was carrying a mile-high crush on Martina.

Jonathan joined him at the railing and inhaled the night air. "You've come up with some harebrained ideas before, but this one takes the cake," he said as if he could read Noah's mind.

Noah glanced at his brother in surprise. "What do you mean?"

"You don't really think I'm after the woman you intend to marry, do you?" Jonathan asked.

Noah shrugged. "Martina's a beautiful, challenging woman. It would be hard for a man not to fall for her."

Jonathan shook his head. "You must be so ga-ga over her that you can't see straight."

Noah resented the implication that he was out of control. "I can see just fine. You were dancing with her, and you two were laughing. Sounded pretty damn cozy to me."

"Ga-ga," Jonathan repeated. "Totally ga-ga. For Pete's sake, Noah, the woman is so pregnant with your baby she looks like you could say boo and she'd have the child on the spot."

"So?"

Jonathan groaned. "Can't you see that she feels totally out of place here in no-woman's-land? If one of us doesn't talk to her a little, she's gonna think we all hate her guts. Adam is convinced her brothers are going to ride over here and try to burn down the house, and Gideon is convinced she's got some kind of voodoo power, since she's able to make you act so crazy."

"Crazy," Noah echoed. "I'm not acting crazy."

"Thinking I'm after the woman who's carrying your baby isn't crazy?" Jonathan asked. "Think about it."

Noah reconsidered and felt a trace of foolishness trickle through. He glanced at Jonathan. "I don't know what to say."

"You don't have to say anything. Love makes fools of us all."

Noah shifted uncomfortably. "For the most part, I've kept a clear head about Martina. I'm committed to her, but I wouldn't say I'm in love with her."

Jonathan laughed aloud. "Well, you'd damn well better be, because nothing else is gonna work with her."

Noah frowned. "What do you mean? You know I've never gotten too worked up over the idea of being in love with a woman. I'm not even sure I believe in it." He felt an odd twinge at his words, as if they didn't adequately cover his feelings on the matter as well as they once did. "Besides," he continued, "Martina and the baby are too important to let emotions cloud what I need to do."

"Hate to tell you this, bro, but your emotions al-

ready have. Maybe your problem is you've been trying to keep your heart out of this.''

Noah fought a wave of uneasiness. ''I still don't
know what the hell you're talking about.''

''Do you really think Martina's the kind of
woman who is gonna respond well to a calculated
play for her?''

''Well, no.'' Noah rubbed the back of his neck in
frustration. ''Maybe not.''

''You know her a lot better than I do, but I've
always thought women were a little like horses.
With some of them, you follow every rule in the
book and it all works out fine. But if you've got a
Thoroughbred, the regular rules won't necessarily
cut the mustard. Sometimes you've got to follow
your gut, your instincts, your heart. It sounds to me
like you've been leading with your head. If you're
gonna get Martina, you might just have to lead with
your heart.''

Noah prized intellect and passion and held little
faith in human emotion. He'd watched too many
people get hurt from too much feeling and not
enough thinking. Jonathan might as well have told
him he would have to jump off a cliff in order to
win Martina.

There'd been no more chapters read from *The
Hobbit* last night, and Martina had tossed and turned
before she'd fallen into an uneasy sleep. When she
awoke this morning, she felt lost. Determined to get

back control of her life, she showered and began to pack. Midway through her task, a knock sounded at the door.

Martina opened it to Noah. ''I'm leaving today,'' she blurted before she fell under his spell and found another reason to stay with him.

His expression inscrutable, he nodded. ''Okay. If you don't mind waiting until lunch, I'd appreciate it. I've got something I need to show you.''

Surprised at his lack of protest, she agreed and felt her sense of loss deepen as he left her room. She sank onto the bed and fought the urge to cry. She looked out the window onto the Coltrane ranch and saw a land that needed flowers, a home that needed a woman's touch. Surely she couldn't be that woman, she thought. Not with all the history between her family and Noah's.

She closed her eyes and the truth pounded her like a relentless tidal wave. Although she had fought it, she was in love with Noah Coltrane, and her love for him was going to hurt her and her brothers. It was right for their baby to have two parents and to experience the privilege of having Noah as a father, but it was wrong for Martina to betray her brothers. Her brothers had loved her when her father had not. Logan loyalty ran deep, and she feared that if she stayed with Noah, she would feel guilty for the rest of her life. More confused than ever, she knew she needed to return to Dallas to make her decision.

By lunchtime, Martina was ready to bolt, but she

made herself bide her time. Noah met her in the living room and led her out the front door. "Patch, make sure you hang around for the delivery," he called. "I'll be back in a little while."

He turned to Martina and offered his arm as they walked down the steps to the truck. "It occurred to me," he said, "that whatever happens between you and me, our child will spend some time on the ranch, and that means you should know a little about it, too."

His acceptance of her plan to leave rubbed at a raw spot inside her. Had he given up? she wondered. She should be relieved, she told herself. Wasn't that what she had wanted?

She listened as he told her about the various buildings and pastures as he drove throughout the ranch. He showed her the new bunkhouse for the fencing and roundup weekends. Although the Logan ranch possessed a more finished look, Martina was impressed with the size and layout of the Coltrane ranch. The unpolished nature of the ranch held the promise and excitement of fresh possibilities.

Noah pulled to a stop in front of a building under construction. "Let's take a look," he said, and helped her out of the truck.

The spacious two-story building boasted a large number of windows and an elegant, but casual Southwestern-style exterior. Walking through the front doorway, she nodded at all the light from the windows. Martina had always preferred plenty of light in her living quarters.

"It's lovely," she said. "What is it going to be?"

"It was originally going to house a new office, but plans change," he said thoughtfully. "Come upstairs."

They climbed the stairs to the second level, which boasted five rooms and large closets. Two of the rooms featured skylights with shades. Noah led her into one of the smaller rooms. "I thought this could be the nursery. When I found out about the baby, I wanted to make a place for both of you here."

Martina's heart stopped. "Oh, Noah, I can't. I...I..."

He pressed a fingertip to her lips. "You can stay and you can go. It won't change what's between us. If we didn't lose it when you left Chicago and stayed away all those months, it's not going to disappear now, no matter how hard you may want it to." He stroked her cheek and held her gaze. "No matter how inconvenient and scary it is for you, I'm not going anywhere."

His words cut through her confusion with swordlike precision. But Noah didn't understand the war going on inside her, jerking her from one side to the other. "I still need to leave," she said in a voice that trembled, despite her best intentions.

"Okay," he said. "Let's go back to the house."

They rode in silence and Martina's tension grew with each breath she took. When they arrived, she noticed an unfamiliar car parked in front of the house. "Visitor?"

"Yep," he said, but didn't explain.

Lost in a sea of conflicting emotions, Martina got out of the truck and went back into the house with the intention of quickly gathering her belongings so she could leave.

Patch met them in the hall with a broad grin. "Delivery was made and your guest is in the den chatting with Jonathan."

"Good," Noah said, and glanced in the living room. He chuckled.

Curious, Martina peeked into the room. "What was the deliv—" She gasped in shock when she saw a baby grand in the middle of the room. "Omigoodness!"

"Yeah, those suckers are pretty big considering they're called babies," Noah said. He glanced carefully at Martina. "What do you think of it?"

Surprised, she walked closer to the piano and shook her head. "It's beautiful. Just beautiful. I didn't know you played."

"I don't," he said, his jaw ticking with discomfort. "But I thought if you wanted to learn, it would be nice to have one available."

Overwhelmed, she gaped at him. "You bought this for me?"

He shrugged and leaned over to touch one of the ivory keys. "I thought it might be a way to make you feel a little closer to your mother."

Martina's chest filled with emotion. Her eyes burned with tears. "But don't you think this is a bit much?"

"I didn't get the impression you'd take a ring," he said, lowering his gaze to hers. "Try it out."

She was so moved she was incoherent. Sitting down on the bench, she tinkered with the keys. "I don't know how to play. How could you do this?" she asked in a voice wobbly to her own ears. "Why?"

"This was an illogical, emotional decision," he said. "You miss the mother you never had. I can't bring her back for you. But maybe I can do something that will make you feel like she's not so far away." He stepped into the hallway. "Hey, Patch, would you bring the visitor in?"

"Visitor?" Martina said, still overwhelmed.

An elderly lady with fluffy white hair entered the room and gave a soft little gasp. "Stars! You look just like Anna."

Confused, Martina looked to Noah for help. "Pardon?"

"This is Helen Lowry and she was your mother's piano teacher when your mom was a little girl. Helen is still teaching piano and she'd be happy to take you on as a student."

One moment ago, Martina hadn't dreamed she could be more overwhelmed, but he'd topped her. "You knew my mother?"

"Most of her life," Mrs. Lowry said with a smile.

"She was a sweet girl who occasionally got into mischief. When she first started taking lessons with me, her mother would dress her in the prettiest little dresses. But Anna liked to climb trees and she was always showing up with skinned knees. She hated the finger exercises I assigned, but soon enough she made friends with the piano. By the time she met your daddy, she had received a scholarship to attend a music conservatory."

Martina felt as if she'd traveled across a desert and found a fountain of the sweetest water on earth. She'd known so little of her mother because her father hadn't wanted to speak of her, and her brothers only knew what little they remembered.

"Did she go?" she asked. "Did she go to the conservatory?"

Mrs. Lowry shook her head. "No. Your daddy bought her a piano and she was as crazy about him as she was her music. When the babies started coming, she was crazy about them, too."

Martina's throat grew tight. "I really don't know if I have any musical ability, but even if I can't learn to play, I would love for you to tell me about my mother."

Mrs. Lowry's eyes softened. "Now don't you worry. I've taught kids who were tone deaf." She patted Martina on the shoulder. "And I'll be happy to tell you all kinds of stories about your mother."

Martina glanced up to find Noah, but he was gone

from the room. She needed to talk to him. She needed to thank him. But how could she possibly?

"We really should begin, dear," Mrs. Lowry said.

Martina blinked. "Begin what?"

"Your first lesson, of course. Let's start with middle C. It's right here," she said, hitting a key. "Now, the proper position for your hands is…"

Martina gamely tried to accept instruction from Mrs. Lowry, but her head was in a whirl. In the past thirty minutes, Noah had delivered one surprise after another. And now, heaven help her, she was attempting to learn to play the piano. Another thirty minutes passed and Mrs. Lowry left, and Martina was staring at the beautiful piano.

"How'd it go?"

Her jaw worked, but no sound came out. She took a calming breath. "I don't know. I may not have my mother's patience with this. Then again, I don't have much patience with anything." She stared at him. He was leaning casually against the doorjamb as if he hadn't just given her a miracle. "Where did you find her?"

"I've known Mrs. Lowry for a long time. I used to cut her lawn. She was one of the few people who gave one of those bad Coltrane boys a chance. When I saw your mother's piano the other day, though, it clicked that Mrs. Lowry might have known her. I gave her a call this morning and…" He shrugged.

She stood and walked toward him. ''Do you have any idea what you've given me?''

''A big piano,'' he said.

She closed her eyes and her heart just overflowed, and so did her tears.

Noah made a sound of alarm and pulled her against him. ''Mrs. Lowry didn't smack your fingers with a ruler when you hit a wrong note or something, did she?''

''No,'' Martina said, laughing through her tears at the ridiculous notion. ''She's the kindest woman.'' Martina shook her head and met his gaze. ''Noah, don't you realize you've just given me a piece of my mother? A piece of her I would never have known without you? I just...'' Her voice broke and she sobbed.

Noah winced. ''Are you sure this is good?''

''Yes!'' she wailed.

''Okay,'' he said in a doubtful voice, and held her as she cried. No one had ever given her such a gift. Although he'd captured pieces of her heart when he gave her little things for the baby, this gift was truly just for her. She would never be the same because of it, and she would never feel the same toward Noah because of it.

''I hate to see you cry,'' he muttered into her hair.

''I hate to see me cry, too,'' she said ruefully, and sniffed. ''But if there's such a thing as a good cry, this is it.''

"Maybe Jonathan was right, after all," he said more to himself than to her.

"Jonathan?" she asked.

He shook his head. "I'll tell you about it another time. Now I need..."

"...for me to kiss you," she said, lifting her mouth to his.

His arms tightened around her. "Something I always need."

Martina kissed him with all the feelings in her heart, all the joy and sorrow for her mother, all the love and desire she had for him.

Through the haze of that long, searching, scorching, wanting, needing kiss, Martina heard the sound of an exaggerated cough. Noah reluctantly drew away and Martina saw all three of his brothers standing in the hall and staring.

"I take it she liked the piano," Jonathan said with a devious grin.

"Don't y'all have anything better to do than watch me?" Noah asked.

Arms crossed over his chest, Gideon looked at Adam. Chugging a canned soda, Adam looked at Jonathan, who grinned hugely. Then all three of their gazes connected with Noah's. "No," they said in cheerful unison.

Noah groaned. "Let's go," he said, urging Martina toward the front door.

"Where are we going?" she asked.

"For a walk."

He led her a short distance away from the house to a small stand of trees where they could enjoy the shade. He tugged her down in the grass to sit between his legs. Martina had the strong, undeniable feeling that she was where she belonged. Not wanting to fight it any longer, she turned in his arms. "You have made it very difficult for me to leave," she told him.

"How?" he asked, his gaze intent.

"By the way you…" She hesitated, not wanting to use the word *love* because he hadn't said he loved her. The knowledge still pinched a vulnerable place deep inside her. But she had never received a more loving gift than what Noah had given her this afternoon. "By the way you care for me."

He ran his hands through her hair and down her arms as if discovering her for the first time. "I will always make it difficult for you to leave," he said, lifting her shirt and baring her pregnant belly to the sun. "Always."

By unspoken agreement, there was no talk of leaving that night, and Noah breathed easier than he had for days. He pushed aside the niggle of discomfort that everything could fall apart in an instant and simply inhaled Martina.

They took their dinner upstairs in his bedroom away from the prying eyes of his brothers. Tonight he didn't want to share. Noah allowed himself to drown in her blue, blue eyes. He drank in her laughter and couldn't stop touching her.

When he read the next chapter of *The Hobbit,* he persuaded her to lift her shirt so he could read against her tummy.

She laughed. "Your voice is vibrating against my skin."

Her laughter was such a turn-on he had a tough time focusing on the story. "I'm giving you a buzz?" he asked, meeting her gaze and wondering how one woman could be so seductive.

"Yeah, you are," she said, the expression in her eyes cranking up his internal temperature.

Noah resisted the urge to toss the book and dive into her. Barely. By the last few paragraphs he was stealing kisses at the end of every other sentence. The book slid to the floor as he rubbed his hands over her belly and felt the movements of the child they'd made.

Martina drew back breathlessly. "I do not understand your fascination with my belly."

"Well, you should," he said, taking her mouth and taunting both of them. "There's a little bit of me and you in there, and it's incredibly sexy knowing I helped put her there."

"Him," she corrected, sliding her hands over his shoulders and chest.

"Her," he argued, removing her shirt in one smooth motion. "I'm fascinated with more than your belly." He unhooked her bra and lowered his head to her breast. Her soft gasp was an intimate velvet stroke. He cupped the turgid peak of her nipple with his tongue, savoring the sensation of her delicate arousal.

He undressed her and dragged his tongue down her belly to her feminine secrets.

"What are you doing?" she asked in a shocked whisper, then, "Omi…ohhh."

He gently took her with his mouth until she was crying out his name. The sound of his name on her lips made him so hard he wondered if he would burst. Moving back up her body, he kissed her and she slid her hand to his erection to stroke him.

Noah sucked in a sharp breath at the pleasure/pain sensation. He tried to still her hands. "You're going to make it hard for me to—"

"That's the idea, isn't it?" she asked in a smoky voice that nearly undid him.

He growled and urged her onto her side. He lay behind her, with his hardness nestled against her bottom, and stroked her breasts.

"What are you…"

Noah pushed against her swollen femininity and she moaned, shifting to ease his entrance. He thrust inside her and they both made sounds of satisfaction. She arched her bottom against him and he pumped inside her silken recesses. "So tight," he muttered, holding on to her hips. "So good."

She clenched around him, and his climax roared through him, taking him by surprise. Her intimate shudders milked his release so that it went on and on, robbing him of breath.

Finally she stopped and, utterly spent, he wrapped his arm around her. After a moment, he felt her begin to cry. She was trying to keep it from him, he suspected, and the knowledge clutched at his heart.

"Martina," he said, rising a little and turning her onto her back. "What's wrong?"

She closed her eyes, but tears still seeped from the corners. "It's nothing. Darn, I've cried more in the last eight months than I've cried in my entire life."

He wiped her tears with his fingers. "What is it?"

She gulped. "I am in such deep doo-doo."

Her distress tore at him. He wanted to fix it. He wanted to spend his life keeping Martina out of deep doo-doo. "Why?"

The power of her gaze shook him. "Because I love you."

Noah pulled her close, wanting to absorb the love she emanated, wanting also to push away the glimmer of fear he saw in her eyes. He slept, embracing her the whole night through. The next day her smile outdid the sunshine and he told her so. The day was so magical he allowed his brothers to share her only at dinnertime.

She surprised him when she talked cigars with Gideon. "How do you know so much about cigars?" Noah asked her.

She shot him a guilty look, but smiled. "I tried a few in college on a dare."

Noah did a double take. "I'm trying to picture this."

"Don't," she said. "I was about as smooth as gravel. Coughed the entire time."

"That's a nasty habit for a woman," Noah said, wondering what other surprises were in store for him.

"It's a nasty habit for anyone," she said sweetly.

"Touché," Jonathan said.

Gideon just threw him a grumpy look.

"I understand you're the best self-educated man in West Texas," she said to Adam, who had been silent and watchful during the entire meal.

"I like to read."

"Did you know there are several programs where you can get a college degree on-line?" she asked.

"No," Adam said, perking up, despite his caution.

"There are several, and many are self-paced, so you can work them around your schedule. I know of a man who completed his law degree in two years."

Adam's eyebrows shot up in surprise. "What's the Web…" He paused, searching for the correct term.

"Web address?" she asked, and he nodded. "I'll write a few down for you and you can check them out."

She was winning them over, Noah thought, and took her hand beneath the table. No surprise there, he thought, catching a private smile she saved just for him. His heart squeezed tight at her revelation last night.

The doorbell rang, and Patch yelled that he would answer it.

"How was your first piano lesson?" Jonathan asked.

"This is going to take some work," she admitted wryly. "I asked her if she would mind fitting in two lessons when she visits."

Jonathan looked confused. "You want longer lessons?"

"No," Martina said with a sly smile. "I thought she could start teaching you."

Noah roared at the poleaxed expression on Jonathan's face. Jonathan stumbled over his protest, but Martina just laughed.

In the middle of her laughter, an angry male voice rang out. "Where's Martina?"

Twelve

The sight of her brothers' angry faces stopped Martina's heart. "Brock," she said, standing, then wondering if her legs would support her. "Tyler."

Brock glanced at the Coltrane brothers with undisguised loathing. "Get your things," he said to her. "We're here to take you home."

"But—"

"But nothing," Tyler said, disdain oozing from his voice. "It's obvious the Coltranes have tricked you again. You just can't see straight when you get around them."

Noah stood in front of Martina in a protective posture. "Now wait just a minute," he said.

"We don't have to wait a second for you. You're the one who caused this trouble from the beginning. If you hadn't gotten her pregnant—" Brock said.

"It takes two to get pregnant," Martina interjected.

"You had to be insane at the time," Brock told her. He looked at her, his face full of disappointment. "You know better."

"Don't give her a hard time," Noah said, his nostrils flaring in anger.

"A little late to be protecting her," Tyler said. "You should have been protecting her when you got her pregnant."

Adam stood. "That's pushing it, Logan."

"Yeah, well, I've just started," Tyler snarled.

Martina's stomach roiled with nausea. She had never seen her brothers so angry. Every nasty quality was coming out now. "Stop it!" she cried. "You're making me sick. You're not even listening."

"This has been coming for a long time," Brock said. "You go get your stuff and we'll take you home."

"Martina may not want to go with you," Noah said.

Brock narrowed his eyes and moved toward Noah. "When it comes to Coltranes, she doesn't know what's best for her."

"You weren't invited on our property," Adam said. "I think you'd better be leaving."

"We're not leaving," Tyler said as he stood toe-to-toe with Adam, "until we take Martina."

"This could get messy," Noah said to her. "I don't want you to see this. Go upstairs."

"I can still hear from up there," she said.

"Let me handle this," he told her.

"There's no *handling* my brothers when they're like this," she whispered, growing more nauseated by the second. "Maybe I should leave."

"Go upstairs," Noah said firmly.

One too many orders for Martina. If her brothers and the Coltranes were stupid enough to come to blows over this, then she wasn't going to stop them. Too upset for words, she left the dining room, grabbed her purse from the end table where she'd left it and headed outside to her car.

The sky was cloudy and angry-looking just like the atmosphere in the house. Martina climbed into the Mustang and secured the convertible top. She started it, then gunned it down the driveway.

She'd known the Waterloo with her brothers was coming, but she hadn't expected it tonight. She couldn't believe the hate on their faces. Since she'd lived with the Coltranes the past few days, she'd gained a new perspective on the family. They were every bit as honorable as her brothers. They struggled to produce more with less. They cared about each other, and she cared about them. Nothing could make her stop loving her brothers, but she still cared about the Coltranes. She just wished her brothers could accept that. She wished they could accept Noah. She wished...a lot of things. Her stomach tightened at how mean her brothers had been.

Tumbleweed rolled across her windshield. She gave a start and glanced at the sky again. The clouds were even angrier, and it was obvious, from all the flying debris, that the wind was picking up. Not the best time for a drive, she thought, and turned on the headlights. She considered turning around, but the thought of returning made her stomach roil again. She couldn't bear to hear her brother's angry voices.

Tightening her hands on the steering wheel, Martina continued to drive until visibility all but disappeared. Wind whipped up, violently stirring dust and dirt. Her already low spirits sank to her feet when realization hit her. She was in the middle of a dust storm. She pulled to the side of the road, stopped and told herself to stay calm.

"Take a breath," she told herself. "Relax."

She inhaled, then felt the distinct sensation of water gushing down her legs. Alarm shot through her. "Oh, no. Houston," she muttered, "we have a problem."

Tyler took a break from hurling insults, and Noah heard the sound of dust and sand striking the window. He frowned, stepping closer to the window. "What the—"

"Noah Coltrane, I want you to stay away from Martina," Brock said.

"No," Noah said, frowning at the gray weather outside. "Not unless Martina tells me to stay away from her, and that won't happen because she's in love with me."

Sudden silence descended on the room. Then Tyler demanded, "She's what?"

"She's in love with me," Noah said impatiently. He had a sinking feeling Martina had not done what she'd been told to do. He rushed to the front door, and although the visibility was poor, he could see that her car was gone. His gut twisted into a knot. "The woman does not take direction well."

"What the hell are you talking about?"

In the distance, Noah could see a fierce dust storm, and Martina was probably right in the middle of it. "Listen," he said, his patience and tolerance shot, "you two might have the time and energy to keep a hundred-year-old grudge going, but I've got more important things to do. Damn," he muttered, feeling his skin grow damp with a cold sweat.

Tyler stepped in front of him and gathered the neck of his shirt in his hands. "What the hell are you talking about?"

Noah felt his brothers move in unison. He gestured for them to stay back. He removed Tyler's hands. "We're not teenagers anymore, Ty. We're not going to fight. There's a dust storm out there and your sister's probably in it."

Alarm widened Tyler's eyes. His gaze shot to the window, then back to Noah. "What do you mean?"

"I mean her little blue Mustang convertible is gone from the driveway and she's probably stuck in a dust storm."

"But we told her to get her stuff," Tyler said.

Noah laughed without humor. "When did Martina follow instructions?"

Realization crossed Tyler's face. "Oh, hell!"

"I'm going after her," Noah said.

"You won't be able to see a damn thing," Adam warned him.

"She's upset. I can't leave her out there by herself when I know she's upset. Anything could happen to her. She's pregnant, for God's sake."

Silence descended again.

"Why didn't she listen?" Brock asked. "I *told* her."

"I think she did listen," Noah said in a dark tone, "all too well. We all gave her an earful, didn't we?"

Her brothers had the grace to look ashamed. Maybe there was hope, Noah thought, but he was too concerned about Martina to give a damn at the moment.

"Take my truck," Adam offered. "But be careful."

"I'll check the opposite direction," Brock said, his face creased with worry.

"Don't get yourself hurt," Noah told Martina's brothers as he grabbed his hat. "She couldn't bear it if either of you got hurt." He ran out the door.

Noah barely cleared the driveway before the dust

whipping against the windshield forced him to adjust his speed to a snail's pace. Noah hated that he hadn't protected her from the ugly scene at the house. He should have found a way to circumvent it. He should have confronted her brothers before now. Seeing their families at each other's throats had probably torn her up inside. The idea of her suffering hurt so much it took his breath away.

With each foot he crawled forward, he prayed she was okay. What if she'd gotten hurt? What if she'd lost control of the car? He began to sweat with outright fear again.

Why hadn't he told her she was the most important person in the world and he didn't know how he could live without her? Why hadn't he told her that he loved her?

Noah knew with every beat of his heart that he loved Martina. Why hadn't he told her?

Berating himself, he continued to drive forward. The wind slowed for a moment and he saw a flash of blue. His heart raced. Her car. He pulled over and got out of the truck, shielding his eyes with his hands. The wind whipped around him in a fury. He reached Martina's car and pounded on the window. The door opened and he quickly scooted inside.

"Noah!" she said, leaping into his arms. "I've been so frightened."

"*You* have been frightened!" he said, holding her tightly as he scolded her. "You should never have gone out in this weather."

He felt her tense. Her breathing quickened. Noah pulled back slightly and studied her. "Are you okay?"

She continued taking slow, shallow breaths. "Yes and no," she finally said.

Noah took in the flush of her cheeks and the strain around her eyes. "Explain that answer."

She gave a weak smile. "My water broke and I'm in labor."

Alarm shot through him. He swore. "We need to get you to a hospital."

Martina shook her head, her face tightening again with another contraction. "I don't think we're going to have time."

Noah fought panic. "You have to slow down."

She looked at him as if he'd lost his mind. *I can't.*"

She couldn't have the baby in the car, he told himself. She couldn't. "How close are the contractions?"

She grimaced and cried out in pain, digging her nails into his palm.

"Close," he said. "Damn." He looked outside. Visibility was zero. He had never felt more helpless in his life, but he had never been more needed in his life.

Martina stared at him, taking quick short breaths. "I'm scared, Noah. What if something bad happens? What if the Logan curse is at work again?"

Her fears scored his heart. "Nothing bad is going

to happen. You're going to have a baby girl and I'm going to be with you every contraction and you and her are going to be fine.'' He said it as much for himself as for her.

Her contraction passed and she drooped against the door. ''I read about this in one of my pregnancy books. Some women have very short labors and get caught off guard. It's rare the first time.'' Her face contorted in another grimace and she began to breathe rhythmically. She held tightly to his hand. ''I wish I had practiced my breathing more. Oh, Noah, it hurts!''

He felt her pain like a knife in his side. ''Focus,'' he said. ''Open your eyes and pick a focal point.''

She squinted her eyes and stared into his. ''Promise me,'' she managed in a ragged voice.

''Promise you what, Martina? I'll promise you anything,'' he assured her, still holding her hand, wanting more than anything to take away her pain.

''Promise me that if I die, you will always love and cherish this child.''

''Honey, you're not going to die,'' he told her, his eyes growing wet with emotion. ''Dammit, you're not going to die.''

''Promise me,'' she implored him.

''I promise,'' he said, then made another oath. ''I love you, Martina. I'm not going to let you die.''

Her eyes rounded at his words. ''You—'' She moaned. ''I want to push.''

Noah alternately swore and prayed. "It's not time, is it?"

"I've got to push!" she yelled, and Noah wasn't inclined to argue.

Two contractions of pushing passed and Noah positioned his hands between Martina's legs. A little head crowned. "She's coming," he said in wonder.

"He," Martina cried. "He's going to look like you." She closed her eyes and pushed again, and the baby's head emerged. The tiny red-faced infant screamed.

"Omigod, she's already yelling," Noah said, trembling at the first sight of his child.

Martina gave one more push and the baby slid out in a whoosh.

"Oh, Lord, it's a girl!"

Martina gaped at him. "It's a girl?"

Noah nodded, tears flowing down his cheeks. "We have a girl. We have a baby girl. Damn," he said, holding her. "What do we do with her?"

Martina sank back against the door. "Put her on my stomach while we decide."

Noah looked around the car for a blanket, but there was nothing, so he stripped off his shirt and wrapped the baby in it. "I don't know what to do with the umbilical cord. Damn, I wish I'd read something about this."

"Even though he's a hardheaded jerk sometimes, this is when it would be handy for Tyler to show up," Martina said. She gazed at their child and touched the baby's tiny fingers. "Oh, Noah, she's beautiful. Isn't she beautiful?"

"Almost as beautiful as her mother," he said, staring with wonder at both of them.

Martina pointed out the window. "Look, the wind has died down."

"Figures," Noah said. "I'm getting you to the hospital."

A Jeep and Gideon's truck pulled alongside them and stopped. Brock and Tyler jumped out of the Jeep, and Noah's brothers rushed from the truck.

Noah opened the window. "You're all officially uncles," he said. "You have a niece."

All five men stared at him dumbfounded. The baby started to cry, and they looked at one another.

Gideon cracked a broad grin. "I'm armed for the occasion," he said, and pulled out cigars.

One week later, on a hot, sunny day, Martina's brother Brock gave her away in marriage to a good-for-nothing Coltrane, who had turned out to be good-for-everything for her. The small gathering included just the two families, who had made peace with the birth of Anna Logan Coltrane. Adam and Brock were discussing cattle, and Tyler expressed an interest in learning to fence with Gideon.

Since last week, Martina had learned a small meteor shower had precipitated the dust storm. That might not have been stars falling over West Texas, but it was close enough to be a sign for her. More importantly, she couldn't imagine not being with Noah Coltrane for the rest of her life. Martina chose a long, ivory, silk empire dress, and Jill had put flowers in her hair. Felicity held the baby while Noah took Martina's hand and said his vows.

"With this ring, I thee wed," he said, his heart in his eyes.

Martina still couldn't believe it. She repeated her vows, then whispered, "Pinch me."

His eyebrows lifted in disbelief. "What?" he whispered back.

"Pinch me," she said. "I can't believe this is happening."

"I can do better than that," he said, then pulled her into his arms and kissed her deeply.

The minister gave a long-suffering sigh, and his lips twitched. "Most people wait, but I can tell you two aren't much on waiting. I now pronounce you husband and wife," he said.

Noah kissed her again, sealing his vows. "I love you," he said.

Her heart turned over. "I'll never get tired of hearing you say that." Noah would never quite understand how his love had healed her of the emptiness she'd felt because her father had been unable to show his love. Martina was determined to spend a lifetime reminding Noah how important he was to her. She glanced around at the happy faces of their families. "I think we've finally done it," she said.

"I think we've learned how to beat the Logan curse."

Tyler and Brock nodded in agreement and walked toward her. They kissed her on opposite cheeks. "I think you sealed it," Brock said.

"And buried a grudge at the same time," Tyler added.

It never failed to bring tears to her eyes knowing that the three men she loved most had made amends.

"How's that?" Noah asked.

"You should know. You're the one who taught me," Martina said, lifting a hand to his cheek. "Love hard, always."

"Always," he promised.

And they always did.

* * * * *

Multi-*New York Times* bestselling author

Nora Roberts

knew from the first how to capture readers' hearts.
Celebrate the 20th Anniversary of Silhouette Books
with this special 2-in-1 edition containing her fabulous
first book and the sensational sequel.

Coming in June

Irish Hearts

Adelia Cunnane's fiery temper sets proud, powerful horse
breeder Travis Grant's heart aflame and he resolves to
make this wild ***Irish Thoroughbred*** his own.

Erin McKinnon accepts wealthy Burke Logan's loveless
proposal, but can this ravishing ***Irish Rose*** win her
hard-hearted husband's love?

Also available in June from
Silhouette Special Edition (SSE #1328)

Irish Rebel

In this brand-new sequel to ***Irish Thoroughbred***, Travis and
Adelia's innocent but strong-willed daughter Keeley discovers
love in the arms of a charming Irish rogue with a talent for
horses...and romance.

Silhouette®
Where love comes alive™

Visit Silhouette at www.eHarlequin.com

PSNORA

SILHOUETTE'S 20TH ANNIVERSARY CONTEST
OFFICIAL RULES
NO PURCHASE NECESSARY TO ENTER

1. To enter, follow directions published in the offer to which you are responding. Contest begins 1/1/00 and ends on 8/24/00 (the "Promotion Period"). Method of entry may vary. Mailed entries must be postmarked by 8/24/00, and received by 8/31/00.

2. During the Promotion Period, the Contest may be presented via the Internet. Entry via the Internet may be restricted to residents of certain geographic areas that are disclosed on the Web site. To enter via the Internet, if you are a resident of a geographic area in which Internet entry is permissible, follow the directions displayed on-line, including typing your essay of 100 words or fewer telling us "Where In The World Your Love Will Come Alive." On-line entries must be received by 11:59 p.m. Eastern Standard time on 8/24/00. Limit one e-mail entry per person, household and e-mail address per day, per presentation. If you are a resident of a geographic area in which entry via the Internet is permissible, you may, in lieu of submitting an entry on-line, enter by mail, by hand-printing your name, address, telephone number and contest number/name on an 8"x 11" plain piece of paper and telling us in 100 words or fewer "Where In The World Your Love Will Come Alive," and mailing via first-class mail to: Silhouette 20th Anniversary Contest, (in the U.S.) P.O. Box 9069, Buffalo, NY 14269-9069; (in Canada) P.O. Box 637, Fort Erie, Ontario, Canada L2A 5X3. Limit one 8"x 11" mailed entry per person, household and e-mail address per day. On-line and/or 8"x 11" mailed entries received from persons residing in geographic areas in which Internet entry is not permissible will be disqualified. No liability is assumed for lost, late, incomplete, inaccurate, nondelivered or misdirected mail, or misdirected e-mail, for technical, hardware or software failures of any kind, lost or unavailable network connection, or failed, incomplete, garbled or delayed computer transmission or any human error which may occur in the receipt or processing of the entries in the contest.

3. Essays will be judged by a panel of members of the Silhouette editorial and marketing staff based on the following criteria:

> Sincerity (believability, credibility)—50%
> Originality (freshness, creativity)—30%
> Aptness (appropriateness to contest ideas)—20%

Purchase or acceptance of a product offer does not improve your chances of winning. In the event of a tie, duplicate prizes will be awarded.

4. All entries become the property of Harlequin Enterprises Ltd., and will not be returned. Winner will be determined no later than 10/31/00 and will be notified by mail. Grand Prize winner will be required to sign and return Affidavit of Eligibility within 15 days of receipt of notification. Noncompliance within the time period may result in disqualification and an alternative winner may be selected. All municipal, provincial, federal, state and local laws and regulations apply. Contest open only to residents of the U.S. and Canada who are 18 years of age or older, and is void wherever prohibited by law. Internet entry is restricted solely to residents of those geographical areas in which Internet entry is permissible. Employees of Torstar Corp., their affiliates, agents and members of their immediate families are not eligible. Taxes on the prizes are the sole responsibility of winners. Entry and acceptance of any prize offered constitutes permission to use winner's name, photograph or other likeness for the purposes of advertising, trade and promotion on behalf of Torstar Corp. without further compensation to the winner, unless prohibited by law. Torstar Corp and D.L. Blair, Inc., their parents, affiliates and subsidiaries, are not responsible for errors in printing or electronic presentation of contest or entries. In the event of printing or other errors which may result in unintended prize values or duplication of prizes, all affected contest materials or entries shall be null and void. If for any reason the Internet portion of the contest is not capable of running as planned, including infection by computer virus, bugs, tampering, unauthorized intervention, fraud, technical failures, or any other causes beyond the control of Torstar Corp. which corrupt or affect the administration, secrecy, fairness, integrity or proper conduct of the contest, Torstar Corp. reserves the right, at its sole discretion, to disqualify any individual who tampers with the entry process and to cancel, terminate, modify or suspend the contest or the Internet portion thereof. In the event of a dispute regarding an on-line entry, the entry will be deemed submitted by the authorized holder of the e-mail account submitted at the time of entry. Authorized account holder is defined as the natural person who is assigned to an e-mail address by an Internet access provider, on-line service provider or other organization that is responsible for arranging e-mail address for the domain associated with the submitted e-mail address.

5. Prizes: Grand Prize—a $10,000 vacation to anywhere in the world. Travelers (at least one must be 18 years of age or older) or parent or guardian if one traveler is a minor, must sign and return a Release of Liability prior to departure. Travel must be completed by December 31, 2001, and is subject to space and accommodations availability. Two hundred (200) Second Prizes—a two-book limited edition autographed collector set from one of the Silhouette Anniversary authors: Nora Roberts, Diana Palmer, Linda Howard or Annette Broadrick (value $10.00 each set). All prizes are valued in U.S. dollars.

6. For a list of winners (available after 10/31/00), send a self-addressed, stamped envelope to: Harlequin Silhouette 20th Anniversary Winners, P.O. Box 4200, Blair, NE 68009-4200.

Contest sponsored by Torstar Corp., P.O. Box 9042, Buffalo, NY 14269-9042.

PS20RULES

ENTER FOR
A CHANCE TO WIN*

Silhouette's 20th Anniversary Contest

Tell Us Where in the World
You Would Like *Your* Love To Come Alive...
And We'll Send the Lucky Winner There!

Silhouette wants to take you wherever
your happy ending can come true.

Here's how to enter: Tell us, in 100 words or less,
where you want to go to make your love come alive!

In addition to the grand prize, there will be 200
runner-up prizes, collector's-edition book sets
autographed by one of the Silhouette anniversary
authors: **Nora Roberts, Diana Palmer,
Linda Howard** or **Annette Broadrick**.

DON'T MISS YOUR CHANCE TO WIN!
ENTER NOW! No Purchase Necessary

Silhouette®
Where love comes alive™

Visit Silhouette at www.eHarlequin.com to enter, starting this summer.

Name:

Address:

City: State/Province:

Zip/Postal Code:

Mail to Harlequin Books: **In the U.S.:** P.O. Box 9069, Buffalo, NY
14269-9069; **In Canada:** P.O. Box 637, Fort Erie, Ontario, L4A 5X3

*No purchase necessary—for contest details send a self-addressed stamped envelope to:
Silhouette's 20th Anniversary Contest, P.O. Box 9069, Buffalo, NY, 14269-9069 (include
contest name on self-addressed envelope). Residents of Washington and Vermont may
omit postage. Open to Cdn. (excluding Quebec) and U.S. residents who are 18 or over.
Void where prohibited. Contest ends August 31, 2000.   PS20CON_R2